Go Fore It!
A Family and Golf Story

By:

Christopher T. Everett

RLE Impel Productions, LLC.
www.goforeitusa.com

Copyright 2021

ISBN: 978-1-7378497-0-4

Cover design by: Kimberly Everett
Library of Congress Control Number: VAU 1-443-709

Edited by:
Kayla Promise
Karen Everett

Contents

Introduction

Go Fore It! is a story about a young man finding and pursuing his passion, which in this case, is the game of golf. At the same time, it's the story of an engaged and hands-on father embracing the fact that his son may not want to follow in his footsteps athletically or in his career choice. Together, with the help of a strong family unit, faith-based community, and wisdom from a trusted elder, they overcome their fear, and each finds happiness for themselves and each other.

In the game of golf, there is a lack of diversity. There are many reasons that account for this lack of representation, some of which are highlighted in this book. The fact remains, golf is a game that offers many opportunities for education, networking, careers, and recreation regardless of gender, age, or race. Due to lack of exposure, many Black and brown people are excluded from these rich opportunities professionally, personally, and economically. If you have not taken the time to get to know the game, make time, you'll be happy you did. Go Fore It!

Lastly, this book highlights many individuals that have pursued their passion to become the first or the best at their craft. As you turn the pages of this book, I invite you to consider your passions; what are you doing to bring them to life? How have family, faith, and self-discipline impacted your ability to pursue your passion? What are you doing to help those around you pursue their passions?

The Basketball Game

It was a night unlike any this town had seen in several years. The Eastway High School gymnasium, home of the Warriors, was fully alive. The concert band set a rhythmic heartbeat for the gym while the home team crowd breathed a jubilant chant into the air to the tune of the Mary J. Blige song, "Real Love." "...E-Dub, I'm talking bout that E-Dub. We came to represent the E-Dub, ...ohh I'm talkin bout the E-Dub." On one side of the court, cheerleaders with voice cones and pompoms added bursts of energy, chanting, "Cougar Pride in the house tonight, Cougar Pride in the house tonight! Go Cougars go Cougars go!" Which was met with opposing chants from the other side of the court of, "Ashes to ashes, dust to dust, we hate to beat you down, but we must, we must!" The energy is electric! The full capacity crowd is all standing and moving side to side as a flowing wave of humanity. On the court, the home team Warriors are fighting to do something they haven't done in years, beat their cross-town rivals on their home basketball court.

There's less than 40 seconds left in this cross-town rivalry game. The Warriors are down 54 to 56 against the Cougars. Sam, who leads the Warriors with 17 points, 7 rebounds, 4 steals, and 6 blocked shots, has just committed his 5th foul and is now the second Warrior to foul out of the game. Coach Floyd turns to Tyler and says, "Tyler, we need you. We're down 2 points and it's their ball. I need you to pressure the ball. If you have an open shot, take it. If not, get the ball to Michael, and he'll take it from there."

Tyler was both excited and nervous. This was the second to the last game of the season, and though he'd played in every game, he hadn't scored a basket. Tyler tore off his purple and white warmup suit, wiped the bottom of his sneakers with his hand, and took a few squats to loosen his legs, before jogging onto the court. The whistle blew, and the referee handed the Cougars the ball to inbound under the Warriors basket.

The Warriors were in a full court press, making it difficult to inbound the ball. Tyler was covering the inbounder. He had his hands up, eyes focused on the player in front of him, and was yelling, "Defense Warriors, defense!" The inbounder spotted an open teammate and leaned to the side to get a better angle for a bounce pass. He let the ball go towards his open teammate, and at the same time, Tyler raised his leg. Bang! The ball hit Tyler's foot, and back out of bounds it went, only running 2 seconds off the clock.

The Warriors crowd gasped. "Coach Floyd clapped and cheered. "Great job Tyler, keep the pressure on him." The referee gathered up the ball, handed it to the Cougar player, and again, he attempted to inbound the ball. Again, the Warriors and Tyler applied pressure. This time, the inbounder found an open teammate near half-court. He cocked his arm to throw the ball, and let the pass go.

Bang! This time Tyler got a hand on the pass. The ball went straight up in the air, which started the play clock again. Tyler jumped to grab the ball, but had to tip it to himself twice to get control of it. Once in his hands, he took his shot, a layup at the goal. Not having the chance to square himself up at the basket, the ball rolled across the rim and off on the other side.

Aggressively, Tyler was the first player in the air reaching for the rebound. He got it and he sprang up to attempt another layup. This time he was square to the basket and had a clear view of the goal. He let the ball go up towards the rim when out of nowhere, the shot was blocked. Immediately, the whistle blew. "Foul 39 Blue, 2 shots," yelled the referee. The gym exploded with excitement, cheers from the Warriors fans, and disbelief from the Cougars fans.

With 26 seconds left on the clock, Tyler walked to the free-throw line to shoot his 2 shots. Tyler took a deep breath. He made eye contact with his mom and dad, who were always at his games, and even his Aunt Asia, who was also in attendance for this big game. She gave him encouraging hand claps and told him, "You can do it, Tyler." He also made eye contact with his coach, who gave him a supportive fist pump.

Tyler took the ball and shot the first free throw. It took 2 laps around the rim before falling off. Missed shot. The Cougar fans let out a sigh of relief, while the Warriors fans, a sigh of disappointment. Tyler, now with his self-confidence starting to fade and his nerves on edge, still held his head up high and prepared for his second shot. Again, he looked to his mom and dad and his coach. He took a deep breath, and away the second shot went. This time, Swoosh! Nothing but net. Tyler had made his first basket of the season, and possibly one of the most important baskets of the year.

This basket brought the Warriors within one point of the Cougars, with 26 seconds on the clock. This time, the Cougars put their tallest player on the baseline to inbound the ball. This player was able to see over Tyler's head and throw the ball over his outstretched arms. He passed the ball to an open teammate over the top of Tyler's head. The player caught the ball, and immediately passed it to another teammate, who was in position to drive to the basket for what could be a game winning shot. Just as the player made his move to dribble to the basket, Steven, a player on the Warriors team, stole the ball.

Steven started advancing the ball up the court and saw Tyler up ahead of him, already in position at the 3-point line. Steven passed the ball to Tyler. With a quick head fake, Tyler allowed the first defender to run past him. He squared his shoulders and let the shot go. The gym went quiet, the buzzer sounded, then the referee blew his whistle. The shot bounced off the rim and fell to the ground. The next sound heard was the referee, "Foul 45 blue, 3 shots." The crowd erupted! Cougars fans vehemently disagreed with the call, while the Warriors fans were elated to still have a chance to win the game.

Tyler, now with the outcome of the game weighing on him, walked to the free throw line to shoot his 3 shots. He looked in the stands at his mom and dad; he looked to his coach. He took the ball, bounced it 3 times, and swoosh. The first shot was nothing but net.

With the game tied at 56-56, the crowd was more alive than any other time that night. Tyler received the ball for his second shot, this time, with the opportunity to win the game. He shot the ball and, Boom!, it hit the backboard and fell to the ground. He'd missed the shot. Again, the crowd reacted.

Now, it was his 3rd and final shot, a last chance for the win. He could feel the sweat starting to build up in the palms of his hands and roll down the side of his face. He could feel his heart beating in his chest louder than the Human Jukebox of Southern University. While his confidence was shaky, he still held his head up high, hoping that if he portrayed confidence, he might start to build some of his own. Ready for his opportunity, he received the ball from the referee, bounced it a few times, took a deep breath, and let it go. Swoosh! Tyler hit the game winning shot! The crowd erupted! This was the first time the Warriors had beaten the Cougars on their home court in 4 years, and the freshmen, Tyler, had hit the game winning shot! Everyone cheered for him and for the big win the team had just earned.

What a night, what a feeling.

After The Game

Tyler's mom and dad were extremely proud of their son and happy for the success he'd just experienced. On the drive home from the game, his mom told him, "I am so proud of the way you played. It was awesome to see how your hard work at practice paid off in such a big game. In anticipation of a victory, I already made one of your favorite meals for dinner. We're having a nice hot beef stew with mashed potatoes."

With a smile, Tyler said, "That sounds great Mom, you know I love your beef stew."

Noticing his smile wasn't the typical big, beautiful smile that would light up any room, or in this case, a dark evening drive home, his mother asked, "What's wrong, are you ok?"

"Yes, I'm fine. Just a little tired... and hungry."

Over dinner, Tyler's dad Ronald, as most proud fathers would, boasted over his son's game winning free throws. He said, "Son, I knew you were going to take care of business. You got in that kid's face with your hands up, eyes focused and determined. I knew you were going to do something special. Oh boy, and when you sprang up to get your own rebound, I nearly jumped up there with you. You went back up strong like you wanted to dunk that thing. I was like, yes, that's my boy! I could tell you didn't have your feet set correctly on the 3 ball, but once he fouled you, I said game over! Tyler is going to put this game away. I knew it! Son, I am just so proud of you." Adding with a big old-school laugh and smile, "You reminded me of myself. Well, except I would have nailed that 3 pointer. I'm just saying, your dad had a mean jump shot back in the day."

Tyler and the rest of the family just laughed, with Tyler saying, "Yes, I know you would have."

Ronald went on to share the names of the other parents and people he'd chatted with after the game. The list included Steven's parents, Sam's parents, the coach of the Warriors, the coach of the Cougars, the school Athletic Director, the newspaper reporter, and he'd even had a conversation with Tyler's Math teacher, Mrs. Star. Tyler's dad loved to interact and speak with people, especially to dote over his children, and on this night, he invited conversations about his son's contribution to the win over the Cougars. However, even Ronald could tell that there was something missing in Tyler's body language. His smile was not as bright as normal, the tone in his voice not upbeat, and he had barely eaten any of his dinner.

After all, he had just helped his team win a big rivalry game and was chowing down on one of his favorite meals. He asked, "What's wrong son, are you down about missing the 3 pointer? If that's the case, don't worry about that, we can work on your jump shot this weekend. Your dad had the coldest jumper in town growing up. My jump shot was cold as ice. I'll help you get right! We can hit the court this Saturday afternoon after your Wilderness Campers service project. I'll have you dropping game winners from half court!" Tyler, seeing the excitement in his dad's face, and enjoying one-on-one time, agreed to the extra practice.

The next day, when the school bus stopped to pick Tyler up for school, the bus driver gave him a high five with a big smile, saying, "Congratulations! The Warriors versus Cougars rivalry is a big deal in this town, and we've lost the last few. But you changed all of that last night. You made it happen! You da man!"

"Thank you," Tyler bashfully said with a smile.

As Tyler walked to his seat, many of his classmates high-fived him, told him congratulations, and did hand gestures to simulate shooting a free throw. One person gave him a hug and their seat on the bus. This was all appreciated by Tyler, but it was also very uncomfortable to him. Tyler was typically a quiet, mild-mannered person, and was unfamiliar with this kind of attention. He had no desire to get comfortable with it either.

When the bus pulled up to the school, the congratulations and high fives continued. In fact, during homeroom, there was an announcement made to congratulate the Warriors basketball team, and Tyler specifically, for his game winning free throws. The entire class and school were all extremely excited, clapping, banging their desks, and chanting, "Warriors, Warriors, Warriors!!"

That day at lunch, Tyler sat with his best friend Ryan, as he'd done since middle school. Ryan and Tyler first met playing soccer together at the YMCA. They became fast friends because of their similar interests in video games, trading cards, and TV shows. They were also in the same Wilderness Campers group and worked together on their advancement projects. Their mothers are also friends. Ryan's mother, Cortney, and Tyler's mother, Joy, both worked as nurses at the same hospital. Tyler and Ryan enjoyed having lunch together because it gave them an opportunity to catch up on the latest episodes of their favorite shows, YouTube and Tik Tok videos, and Wilderness Campers projects.

Today like most other students at the school, Ryan was excited for the win last night. Ryan was also happy for his friend. Knowing that Tyler hadn't scored in any of the other games, seeing him hit the game winning shots added to the excitement. Tyler appreciated the compliments and excitement from his friend; it made him smile, and he was happy to help bring this type of energy to the school. Tyler understood the significance of the game, how long it had been since they beat their rivals, and the fact that he got to contribute to that win. However, for some reason, he just wasn't as excited about it as everyone else.

Tyler didn't want to spend his lunch period discussing the game. He'd had heard enough about the game. He was more interested in talking about this weekend's service project. The Wilderness Campers were going to be serving a hot breakfast at the local homeless shelter. This was the third time Tyler was getting to participate in this project, and he was looking forward to it. Being a very caring person, and having genuine concern for the well-being of others, he really felt connected to this type of service project. Ryan usually participated in the group's hot meal service projects too, but he would be missing this one. Ryan shared with Tyler, "I'll have to miss this weekend. I have my golf lesson this Saturday, and I'll be getting the chance to play on an actual golf course this week. I hate that I have to miss the service project, but I'm over the moon excited about getting to play on a golf course. I've spent a lot of time learning the basics at the driving range and riding along with others on the golf course, but now, I've tested and actually get to play on the golf course myself.

Tyler had heard Ryan speak about his golf lessons in the past, but now was seeing even more excitement from Ryan about golf, which made him more curious. He said, "Nice, tell me more about your golf lessons. When are they? And what is so exciting about playing on a golf course?"

"My lessons are on Wednesday evenings and Saturday mornings. I find golf personally challenging. I like learning new skills at the driving range, practicing, and getting better at them. I remember when I first started taking lessons, I would swing and miss hitting the ball on at least half my strokes. My coach would consistently work with me to keep my head down, bend my knees, keep my arm straight and see the club making contact with the ball. After each stroke, my coach would give me feedback, 'Ryan, you lifted your head that time. You turned your shoulders. Perfect! You made good contact on that one, didn't it feel good?'

Then, I got to the point that I could consistently make contact with the ball, but I would never know where the ball would end up. I'd hit some balls to the left, a ton to the right, and every once in a while, I would hit it straight ahead. My coach would give me feedback about my hand positioning and grip. Like, Ryan, you're holding the club too tight, too loose, too far away from your body, or the club face is open. When I corrected myself, he'd say, 'Perfect! Look at that shot, right down the middle. That was great Ryan, do it again.'

Then, I needed to learn my clubs. There are drivers, wedges, woods, irons, and putters, so many. Different clubs hit the ball different distances and can help you get out of different situations. I find the game very rewarding of the hard work I put into it. It is fulfilling to me. At times like now, getting to reflect on where I started, and this weekend getting to see how the skills I have developed will play out on the golf course. Lastly, my mom pointed out to me that many of the same things I am learning from golf, I can apply to my schoolwork and life."

Tyler, now hanging on Ryan's every word and sharing in his excitement, asked, "How can you apply golf to schoolwork and life."

"It's like this, in order to consistently hit the ball and hit it straight, I had to study my mistakes and practice. In order to get an "A" on that last math test we took, I had to study my notes from class, and work on some practice problems. My coach, or my mom in this case, would review my work and give me feedback."

"Oh, I get it. That makes sense, but how does it relate to life?"

"Ok, here is another example. In golf, you need to know the course and the layout of the fairway, so you know what club to use, and you can prepare properly. The same with Wilderness Campers campouts. We need to know how many people are going, what the weather will be, and our plan in case there are obstacles or danger. Golf has also helped with my self-confidence. I know there's nothing I cannot accomplish with the right amount of focus, effort, and preparation. And it's a really fun game. I get to compete against myself to get better, and play with others for fun. Tyler, you would love golf. You should come take lessons with me. Then we can be golf buddies too."

At this point, Tyler was leaning in towards Ryan with a big, excited smile on his face, 100% ready to sign up for golf. "Definitely, I want to sign up. I'm going to talk to my parents about it tonight at dinner. Getting to be golf buddies would be dope. Oh, wait! I have the Wilderness Campers project this Saturday. Maybe I'll be able to come next week. I'm still going to talk to my parents about it tonight. Golf sounds awesome. I don't know why I haven't asked you about golf before."

That night at dinner, each family member shared about their day. When it was Tyler's turn, he shared about the attention he received about the game, including the bus driver's comments, the way all of the kids on the bus interacted with him, and how the kid he barely knew gave him his seat. However, he was most excited to share about the golf lessons Ryan talked about during lunch.

Tyler said to his parents, "I'd like to go to golf lessons with Ryan this Saturday. What he said about golf sounds really interesting and I want to try it out."

"Don't forget you have the Wilderness Campers service project Saturday morning, and we're working on your jump shot in the afternoon," Ronald said

"Yes, I remember, but I still really want to try taking golf lessons."

"Tyler, I am supportive of you trying something new, and golf would be fine, but you have a lot on your plate. If we want to try golf, it will have to wait until after basketball season," Joy told Tyler.

"Also, after basketball season, you typically help me out more around the shop. I don't want you to miss too much time in the shop. It'll be yours one day and I want you to be well prepared to continue the business. You need to learn from your own experiences, not just what someone tells you or what you read in a book. You have a real opportunity for hands-on learning at an early age that most people don't get. If you're going to add another activity, we have to discuss how you plan to balance all of your responsibilities, including schoolwork being your first priority."

"When Ryan was telling me about golf and the lessons, he told me about how golf has helped him to better prepare for school and life. So, while this may seem like adding one more thing to my already full plate, it could really be helping me to add more of the structure to balance my responsibilities."

His parents looked at each other and smiled at their son's clever way of trying to make his point. Even Chloe had to smile at her brother's creativity in trying to make his case. While Tyler wanted to go this weekend, he knew his parents were right. He had a lot on his plate, and his parents had always taught him to give 100% to anything he did, and to not be a quitter. The Wilderness Campers were expecting him this weekend, and basketball season ended next Thursday. That meant the following Saturday was a better time to start a golf lesson.

That Saturday, after his Wilderness Campers project, Tyler and his dad spent at least 3 hours in the driveway shooting hoops. They practiced dribble drills with the right hand, drills with the left hand, and drills with multiple basketballs. For shooting drills, they practiced by visualizing shots and focusing on keeping their elbows in on jump shots. They practiced an array of shots: lay-ups, trick shots, and bank shots. They played one on one, and Tyler's favorite; they played horse. They both had an enjoyable afternoon. Tyler learned a few new things, and most importantly, he got to spend additional time with his dad.

Ronald loved spending quality time with his son, and getting to play basketball for hours. It was a great day for both father and son. At dinner that night, when it was their turn to share about their day, Tyler talked about the good work they'd done as a part of their Wilderness Campers project, then talked for several minutes about the time he spent with his dad, practicing basketball. During Ronald's turn to share, he highlighted the time he got to spend with Tyler sharpening his basketball skills. Joy shared that she and Chloe enjoyed watching their guys have so much fun playing basketball in the driveway. Joy knew what a blessing it was for Tyler to have Ronald be so hands-on with him, and truly pour his energy and knowledge into him. She knew her guys were awesome and that made her smile. It was truly a great day for their family.

In the next week, Tyler had his last two basketball games of the season. Though he played 20 minutes, had 5 steals, 6 rebounds, 2 blocked shots, and 3 assists; he again didn't score any points.

"Congratulations on a great freshman season. It was great watching the way you stepped up your level of play at the end of the season. It's always about making progress, and that's what you did over the course of the season. I'm very proud of you son!"

"Thanks, Dad. I wish I could have scored more points this season."

"Son, I know scoring feels good, and it's for sure the quickest way to get noticed, but keep in mind there's only one ball, everyone can't be the leading scorer. There have been a lot of basketball greats who impact the game without scoring. These playmakers were terrific defenders and effort players. They weren't focused on lighting up the scoreboard. Think about players like Dennis Rodman, Kendrick Perkins, Draymond Green, Rudy Gobert, and my two HBCU favorites from Virginia Union University, Charles Oakley and Ben Wallace. I call those kind of players grinders, and every team needs at least one, but they are hard to find in today's offensive-minded game. Son, you are on a great path. If you keep working at it, you can do really well in this sport. Like anything worth having, you'll have to work hard at your craft to be successful at it, but you can be great at it."

"Thank you, I appreciate the encouragement and lessons. I love you, Dad." Tyler said with a smile as he hugged his dad.

"I love you too, son."

That night at dinner, Joy expressed how proud of Tyler she was. "You got a lot of playing time for a freshman, and you were a real contributor to the success of the team. You did really well for yourself. Hey, you have turned Chloe into a big basketball fan at 2 years old; out there cheering her brother on. Speaking of Chloe, Ronald, she somehow learned how to use your ratchet to tighten the screws on her bed." Joy said with a big laugh, "I have no idea how she did it, but she did and I am not asking any questions."

Ronald said, "I am not sure if I should be proud or concerned, so I will just say nice work, Chloe." However, Ronald was still gushing over his son, and his basketball success. Tyler was appreciative of the basketball praise, but he was really looking forward to the opportunity to try the game of golf. Although Ronald was noticeably less excited about golf, since he and Joy had already agreed to let Tyler try the lessons, they were supportive of him trying this new sport now that basketball season was over.

As the family finished up from dinner, Joy said, "Tyler, this would have been the weekend you and Chloe spend the night with your Aunt Asia. Since you'll be attending your golf lesson Saturday morning, instead of spending the night with Aunt Asia on Friday night, you and Chloe can spend the night on Saturday and come home after church on Sunday."

"Yes! We still get to spend the night at Aunt Asia's house. I always look forward to spending time at her house, and I'll get to tell her about my first golf lesson."

The First Golf Lesson

The day had finally come. Tyler was about to take his first golf lesson. His mother had to work that day, so his father took him for his lesson. Although Asia would be picking up Chloe on the way to pick up Tyler from his lesson for their sleepover, Ronald decided to attend the full practice. It was Tyler's first experience with golf; he wanted to meet the coach, and see what these lessons were all about. When they pulled up to the practice range, Tyler immediately spotted his friend Ryan among all of the many kids there on the range. Ronald allowed Tyler to hop out of the car to go meet up with Ryan.

Once parked and walking over to the range, Ronald felt a rush of emotions. He began to reflect back on his own experiences growing up, and what little he knew about golf. He didn't have any personal experience playing golf and didn't know anyone who did. To him, golf was always considered a rich White man's sport, and Black people were not welcomed. In fact, most of the well-maintained private country clubs and golf courses did not allow Black people to be members or even play the course as the guest of a member. This was not because they weren't talented enough or qualified, it was simply because they were Black (men and women).

While he had never played the sport, Ronald knew some history about golf. He knew it was as recent as 1961 that Charlie Sifford became the first Black man to earn a PGA Tour card, which allowed him to compete and earn money in PGA tournaments with golfers who were considered the best in the country. It was another 14 years later, in 1975 when Lee Elder became the first Black man invited to play in the Masters tournament. As recent as August 1990, the week that the PGA Championship was scheduled to be played at Shoal Creek Golf and Country Club, that this invitation-only private golf club allowed its first Black honorary member, Louis J Willie. This honorary induction was in response to civil-rights groups threatening to protest, sponsors rescinding their backing of the tournament, and the PGA of America considering moving the PGA Championship away from the club.

It was also after the club's founder, Hall Thompson, was quoted by the *Birmingham Post-Herald* as saying, "We have the right to associate or not to associate with whomever we choose. The country club is our home and we pick and choose who we want. I think we've said we don't discriminate in every other area except the Blacks." Despite his statement, Thompson's compromise to allow a Black man an honorary membership was enough for the PGA Championship to continue as scheduled. However, it was another 6 years, in 1996, before Shoal Creek allowed a Black man to join and obtain full membership benefits. As a result of the backlash and potential loss of revenue from the controversy surrounding the August 1990 championship event, the PGA of America issued a statement that they would pay more attention to the membership policies of potential tournament sites.

Soon after this statement, in September 1990, Ron Townsend was named the first Black man to become a member of the Augusta National Golf Club, home of the Masters. All of this unfavorable history, and now my son is here about to take lessons in the hope of playing this game that has done so much to remain separate and unequal. Ronald wasn't sure if the emotions he felt were anger for what had been accepted for so long, or excitement for the progress being made and the new opportunities now afforded to his son. Nonetheless, he pushed forward and embraced being present and supportive of Tyler. He could take the time to understand what it was he was feeling later.

Ronald made his way over to where Tyler and Ryan were lined up, waiting for their lesson. He found a nearby area with seating that already had a few parents there. Ronald introduced himself and pointed out his son, the other parents did the same. There were roughly 20 kids attending this golf lesson. They were all situated based on experience levels: beginner, intermediate 1, intermediate 2, and experienced. There was one instructor for every 2 golfers.

Ronald looked to his right and left, he saw kids from various racial and ethnic backgrounds, all there taking lessons together. He saw instructors engaged in teaching the mechanics of the game to kids who were focused on learning. He saw golf balls flying left and right, near and far. It was a lot for him to take in and process, but the fact that it seemed Tyler was enjoying himself forced him to find a way to look past it.

When the lesson was almost over, Ryan's father, Mark, was there to pick him up. Ronald and Mark got a chance to speak for a few minutes before the kids walked over. "Mark, do you play golf?" Ronald asked.

"I do now. You know when we were younger, brothers didn't play golf. We used to refer to it as the White people game! However, after Ryan started taking these lessons and I saw how much he liked it, I decided to start learning the game too. I thought it would be a special moment for us to be able to play together one day."

"Oh man, I know what you're talking about. I have never set foot on a golf course. They didn't want us out there, and I didn't want to be out there. I'd take a round ball and a hoop any day, not hit a funny-looking little white ball as hard as I can and walk around all day in the hot sun looking for it."

"Yeah, I know what you're talking about. I played a little basketball, but football was more my thing. Either way, I couldn't care less about golf."

"You know, I felt a little uncomfortable even coming out here today. But I guess I'll have to get used to this if Tyler continues to play. I may even have to take a page from your book and learn the game myself."

"You have to give it a try, you might find you like it. I was definitely surprised that I liked it once I learned it."

"You might be right. I may find that I like it too. However, if Tyler ends up liking it, I'll have to find a way to prepare him for the situations he may find himself in with people that don't respect him simply because of the color of his skin."

"Good point. I need to tackle that subject with Ryan before too long, too."

At that time, Asia walked up to Mark and Ronald with Chloe. Ronald introduced them and they exchanged hellos. Shortly after, Tyler and Ryan came skipping up to Mark, Ronald, and Asia. Tyler gave his aunt a big hug, and with sheer excitement, told his dad, "My first golf lesson was great! The coach said I'm natural. I think I am going to really enjoy playing golf."

"Yes, Tyler is really good. He did much better than I did on my first lesson. He'll be getting to play on the golf course with me in no time." Ryan said.

"We're going to be golf buddies real soon!" Tyler exclaimed.

"Yes, golf buddies soon!"

Ryan then said to his dad, "Are you ready? They're about to leave to head over to the golf course. I have a 1:00 tee time with the 3 guys over there," and he pointed across the range. Tyler gave Ryan a high five and said, "Good luck out there. I hope I get to join you soon." Tyler then turned to his dad and aunt and started telling them all about his golf lesson. How he learned the proper way to hold his club, the mechanics of the swing, and the names of the different clubs. He said it felt really good swinging the club and making contact with the ball. He said he was looking forward to his next lesson and getting better with his golf game.

Asia had no clue what any of the stuff he was talking about meant but could tell her nephew was truly excited. She said, "Come on, let's get in the car and you can finish telling me all about it.

Tyler said, "Okay, Aunt Asia." He gave his dad a big hug and said, "Thanks for signing me up and bringing me to golf today. I am glad we were able to fit it into my schedule. I'll finish telling you all about it tomorrow after church."

Ronald returned the hug and told Tyler, "I'm glad you enjoyed golf. We still need to discuss how this will work with you being able to help out at the shop. We'll make it work. Enjoy your time with your aunt." Ronald then gave Chloe a kiss on her forehead and said, "I love you. You have a good time with your Aunt Asia as well."

Tyler, Asia and Chloe got into the car heading to Asia's house. Tyler talked about his experience at his golf lesson all the way home, including during their stop along the way to Boston Market to pick up dinner. It was clear to Asia that he was very excited about golf, and while this was just his first lesson, Tyler had real passion around this sport. Asia's feelings and perspective toward golf were not as pronounced as her brother's, but she did know a little bit about the history of golf, and felt it was important for Tyler to know it too.

Aunt Asia

Asia is Ronald's baby sister and to the kids, she is known as their cool Auntie. Asia loves her niece and nephew. She spoiled them both rotten by always cooking their favorite foods, taking them on fun trips, teaching them new things, and exposing them to new experiences. Asia was a well-traveled, university graduate, with multiple degrees, work certifications and designations. She truly lives by the YOLOSWN mindset (You Only Live Once So Why Not). This mindset often drove her big brother batty, but it worked for her. She also had a passion for her history and passing that history on to her niece and nephew. She was always excited to share with her niece and nephew, her knowledge of African-American history, Historically Black Colleges and Universities (HBCUs), and Greek life within those institutions of higher learning. She'd given her niece Greek toys, and recommended books for Tyler to read and discuss with her. Some of the books that she and Tyler had already read and discussed included learning about the middle passage, the Divine 9, and HBCU greats like Rev. Dr. Martin Luther King Jr. – Morehouse College, Justice Thurgood Marshall and Langston Hughes – Lincoln University, Julius Chambers – North Carolina Central University, and United States Representative John Lewis and Nikki Giovanni – Fisk University among many others.

Asia enjoyed sharing the lives and accomplishments of these successful HBCU graduates with Tyler, and looked forward to doing the same with

Chloe when she's older. She appreciates the historical significance of HBCUs and wants her niece and nephew to be well informed kids, and make the best decision for themselves when the time came. Also, who didn't love a good HBCU homecoming football game, halftime show, and cookout? What a GREAT time! By way of these interactions and experiences, Tyler and Asia developed a relationship where he had become comfortable confiding in her. When situations came up that he wasn't sure how to handle or wasn't ready to discuss with his mom and dad, he would discuss with his Aunt Asia. She was proud of the relationship they had and very protective of it. She knew how important it was for him to have someone that he felt comfortable sharing these important life situations with, and who could actually help him with the situation, including how to address it with his parents.

When they arrived at Asia's house, everyone got cleaned up for dinner. Chloe washed her hands and prepared herself too. They sat around the table and Tyler prepared a small plate for his sister with mashed potatoes, corn, and green beans. He had the same in addition to 3 chicken legs and a wing. This drew a comment from Asia, "Wow Tyler, your golf game must have made you work up an appetite. That is a lot of food. Are you going to eat all of that?"

"Yes, I guess I am pretty hungry, and I really like Boston Market."

"Well eat up and enjoy."

Asia reached for the breast, and added a few fixings to her plate. She looked across the table and said, "So, Nephew Tyler, you seem to really like golf. You've been talking about it all afternoon."

"Yes, I really do. I know I have a lot to learn, but I really like what I've seen so far."

"What is it about golf that you like so much, you've only had a club in your hand for one morning?"

"I know it's only been one morning, but I felt connected to it. I didn't have to worry about if I made a mistake, was that the right play to run, or is my teammate going to pass me the ball. With golf, like the coach said, I'm playing against myself. I get out of it what I put into it. I felt a type of freedom and creativity on the range that I enjoyed. Even though I didn't hit the ball as well as Ryan today, I know with practice, I'll be able to hit it like he does, and I'll get to go to the golf course as well."

Asia smiled and nodded her head, then asked Tyler, "A few weeks ago, you hit a few game winning free throws in your rivalry basketball game. You helped the Warriors win a really big game, but I do not remember you talking about that nearly as much as you're talking about one morning of golf. Why is that?"

Tyler stopped chewing for a moment, looked up as if in thought, then looked back at Asia and said, "I don't know."

"There has to be a reason, I'm sure there is a reason. What was that thought you seemed to have just then?"

Knowing that his aunt wasn't going to settle for the answer that he had just given her, he knew he had to give her a better answer, an honest answer. He stopped eating, put his fork on the plate, looked up at his aunt, and said, "I am not really that into basketball. I mean, I am pretty decent at it, and just a few days ago, dad was telling me about some of the basketball greats that were great defenders and hustle players, but not big scorers. He calls them grinders, and he said my game is like theirs and I could go far.

I know he believes in me, and he loves the game, but I don't think I do. You know how you, mom and dad always say that you have to work hard to perfect your craft, and that you get out of things what you put into them? Well, I just don't know that I want to work that hard at basketball, it's not my thing. I know dad loves the game. I like playing in the driveway with him. I've seen his trophies. I know he was great at it. I'm his son so I should be great at it too, but it just doesn't excite me. Is that bad?"

Asia, having already known that Tyler wasn't as into basketball as her brother, was happy to finally hear him say it out loud. She wanted to assure Tyler that there was absolutely nothing wrong or bad about him not loving basketball the same way. She told him, "Basketball was Ronald's thing. I know he loved it. I grew up having to hear him bouncing a ball 24/7. Ronald loved the game and would be ready to play at a moment's notice.

I've seen that look in his eye when he was able to go outside and shoot baskets or play in a big game. That's how I knew that you didn't share that same passion and love for basketball, and that's ok. Of course, your dad wants to pour into you and help you be the best you can be at basketball, if that is the sport you want to play. If not, he'll support you and give you all he has to give in whatever you decide to put your heart into, and it will be ok."

"Are you sure he won't be upset? I don't want to disappoint him, and I still want to play pickup games, but I just want to do it for fun."

"I am 100% positive you will not, and could not, disappoint your dad. And good luck keeping him away from a good pickup game."

Tyler, feeling better about having gotten that weight off of his shoulders, continued eating his Boston Market dinner and looked forward to the evening movie they would stream that night.

Ronald's History

That night, with the children at Asia's house, Ronald and Joy got to enjoy a dinner at home with just the two of them. Wanting to maximize their time, instead of cooking, Ronald and Joy ordered delivery from their favorite Chinese restaurant. Over dinner, while enjoying their beef and broccoli, teriyaki chicken, and egg rolls, Joy asked Ronald, "How was Tyler's first golf lesson?"

"I really didn't know what to expect with taking Tyler to the golf lesson. I didn't know anything about golf growing up, it was the rich White people's game. They would let you caddie for them, but they were not about to let us play on their courses. When you were allowed to play, it wasn't on their golf course. You had to play at one on the other side of town, that didn't look anything like theirs, and was not as well maintained as theirs. I guess I had all of those thoughts bouncing around in my mind when I walked up to the range, and I had this weird feeling that just stuck with me for a while. Honestly, I am still thinking about it.

However, Tyler loved it! I mean the boy absolutely loved it. I hate to say it out loud, but I think he enjoyed one golf lesson more than he enjoys playing basketball. I could see it in his eyes. I don't get it. Of course, I want him to love basketball, I know basketball. I can teach him the game and he could be really good at it. It could pay for his education. He would also have to deal with a lot less resistance playing basketball versus this golf stuff. I can't help him or teach him anything about golf; he'll be on his own with that. I'm going to have to figure out how to help him realize his potential with basketball."

"I know, I was surprised when he came home talking about golf too. It was just one lesson, and it is new to him, no need to read too much into it yet. But, if he wants to stay with it, we'll figure out how to prepare him and ourselves for it together. You know I have your back; we'll support each other with how to handle our feelings."

That night, Ronald and Joy reflected on their life together. More specifically, on Ronald's journey, and the life changing opportunity that led to who they are, and where they are today.

Ronald was a star basketball player for his high school team. He still holds several scoring records, was the defensive player of the year for his conference, twice, and was a varsity letter athlete all four years of high school, in basketball and track. Ronald was loved by all of his teachers and the student body, including his long-time girlfriend, Joy. Even the alumni loved Ronald, especially since he had led the school to victories against their cross-town rivals all four years he'd played. In addition to being a great athlete, Ronald was an all-around good person and a great student, graduating with honors and in the top 5% of his class.

With all of his athletic talent and academic success, Ronald would have been a joy to have on any college campus, and could have excelled as a collegiate student athlete. However, his family did not have the money to send him to college and were not aware of how to pursue scholarships or grants to help offset the cost. In addition, Ronald did not realize the value of meeting with his high school guidance counselor to discuss options for continuing his education after high school. Instead, as a teenager, Ronald worked at a local service station called, "Joe's Automotive Service." At that time, his main responsibilities were pumping gas, checking tire pressure, and cleaning windshields.

As he grew older, his scope of responsibilities began to expand. As Ronald was able to spend more time at the station after school and on weekends, he was soon trusted to drive cars into the garage bays. This gave him the opportunity to learn how to drive manual shift cars, old beaters and high-end sports cars. He also learned to do oil changes, tire rotations, and state inspections. Next up were tune ups and simple engine repairs. Ronald soon attended and graduated from technical school for auto mechanics and earned his way to become the Master Mechanic at Joe's Automotive Service.

One morning, Joe Stallworth, the owner of Joe's Automotive Service, called Ronald into his office. Joe shared with Ronald that after owning the business for 35 years, he was going to put the station up for sale. He said that his health was not good. He was tired and could no longer keep up with the demands of the station. He told Ronald that he would like for him to be a part of the sales process and meet the new owner before the sale is completed. He ended the conversation by letting Ronald know that he has not shared this with the other employees yet, but wanted to tell him first because he has been his longest standing and most reliable employee. With a slightly curious yet excited grin on his face, Ronald expressed appreciation for the advanced notice. Knowing that Joe had been laboring more and more each of the past few years to get the work done, he congratulated Joe on his impending retirement.

With an array of emotions evident in his voice, from excitement for a new opportunity, to nervousness and compassion for not getting to continue working with his friend and mentor, Ronald called his wife to tell her not to cook tonight. He wanted to take her out to dinner instead.

During dinner, Ronald told Joy the news that Joe was going to sell the business. They had been saving all of their extra money for just an opportunity like this. Since earning his Master Mechanic certification, his goal was always to own his own shop. Based on his plan he felt they needed another 3-5 years to really be ready, but opportunity was knocking now.

Joy was a very grounded and supportive person. She knew how important owning his own business was to her husband, and she knew he could do it. Just then she was reminded of a conversation she'd had with a co-worker about business loans supported by the Small Business Administration (SBA). These are business loans intended to help people start new businesses or grow existing ones. She shared this information with Ronald and reminded him that she had additional money saved in her retirement account, if needed. They were planning to use some of that money to buy a house, but since their timeline for buying a business was moved up, the money might be needed now. She reaffirmed to him that she loved him, and she believed in him.

That night, Ronald went online to read up on business lending, specifically SBA supported lending options. Ronald was able to start the application process that night from home. Exactly one week later, Ronald received his conditional approval for his SBA backed loan. That night, instead of going out for dinner, Joy prepared Ronald's favorite meal of salmon, spinach, and jasmine rice.

The next morning, with his chest full of pride and his mind racing with every emotion from excitement to self-doubt, Ronald drove to work. Upon his arrival, Joe asked him to come into the office; he had something he wanted to discuss with him. Knowing what the conversation was the last time Joe called him to the office, Ronald hoped he had not missed his opportunity to buy the service station. Once in the office, Joe told Ronald that he had received an offer to purchase the station the night before. Overcome with disappointment, Ronald said, "What? Wait, you can't sell it to them." Joe, confused, and somewhat concerned about Ronald's reaction said, "Ronald, I told you I would have you meet the new owner before I closed on a sale. You are a great person and a hard worker. I am sure you will get along just fine with the new ownership. What's the problem? I have never seen you react this way."

At that point, Ronald said he wasn't upset because of the potential new owner, he was sure they were fine people. He was disappointed because he wanted to buy the station himself. Joe was surprised because he didn't know Ronald had a desire to own the shop. He told Ronald, "You've worked here with me longer than anyone else, I would love for you to take over the business. But how would you afford this place?"

Ronald explained that he had been saving up for this type of opportunity, as well as working with his bank to secure a loan, which he was approved for the previous day. Joe was completely caught off guard by Ronald's proposition, but he was more than happy to turn the business over to his best worker providing they could agree on a good purchase price. Within days, they had an agreed-upon price, and three weeks later, the sale was complete. It included a lump sum payment to Joe and a 5-year retirement payout. They shook hands. Joe handed Ronald the keys, and he drove off into retirement saying, "Florida here I come."

Ronald, now owner of the newly renamed RLE Full Service Automotive, set out to make changes to improve the shop, as outlined in his business plan. Part of the changes included expanding the shop to add additional garage bays. This allowed him to hire 1 new mechanic, and 1 additional service tech. Both of whom he hired from the local automotive technical school. Hiring directly from the school helped these new graduates gain valuable experience and allowed Ronald to better manage his payroll expenses.

Now, with the additional workers and garage bays, Ronald focused his attention on building relationships with local businesses to manage the service and maintenance work for their fleets. He reached out to and met with the local used car dealers, two rental car companies, a couple of landscaping companies, and the police department. Ronald was able to successfully increase the volume of business and revenue the shop produced. This was important because it allowed him to make on-time payments to Joe, and on his SBA loan. In addition, Ronald was also able to rebuild the family savings account and house down payment money ahead of plan.

Ronald, a humble man, had always been proud of the work he'd done at his shop, the life opportunities the shop has created for his family, and the people he'd been able to help and employ along the way. His dream was now to be able to hand the business over to his son and keep the shop in the family for the next generation. However, Ronald feels that dream may be slipping away. It seems that Tyler is not interested in basketball, or working at the shop, his new primary focus appears to be golf.

Joy understood her husband's concerns. She shared his concerns about the potential challenges her young Black son might face in a sport dominated by White men, with a lack of representation of Black faces. However, as a mother, she was supportive of her children having and chasing their own dreams and happiness. She also knew that Tyler was not in love with the game of basketball, and she questioned his interest in the automotive business. She was there to see how hard Ronald worked to build the business. How many long hours he put into running the business by day and studying for his certifications at night. Sure, it would be fantastic for their son to take over the business and continue to grow it and keep it in the family, but that has to be his dream, not the one that they pressure him into. Joy's focus was for her children to become well-rounded, intelligent, and productive adults. What productive looks like for them, they would need to define for themselves.

That night, Joy simply said to Ronald, "Tyler is still young and it's good that he is still open to new experiences, and embracing something new. This was just one lesson. We'll see how long the excitement lasts, and where it goes. Either way we will support him, and we'll deal with it."

Ronald, still unsure about all this, deeply exhaled as he settled into his favorite seat on the couch with Joy right by his side. They both relaxed their minds and made it a wine and movie evening for the rest of the night.

Let's Go To Church

On the way to church Sunday morning, Tyler realized that the next day was a holiday, and that he might be able to spend the extra time with his aunt instead of going back to his house after church.

Tyler asked Asia, "Do you have plans for after church?"

"No, why do you ask?"

"Oh, do you have plans for the holiday tomorrow?"

Already knowing the answer to her question, Asia asked him, "Why do you ask?"

"Well, I was thinking that since tomorrow is a holiday, and you have no plans this afternoon or tomorrow, maybe Chloe and I could stay with you tonight after church?"

"Sure, I'm fine with the two of you staying tonight, as long as your mom and dad are fine with it as well. You'll need to ask them after church service today." Confident that his parents would be agreeable, Tyler sat back in his seat and gave a good fist pump and smile. He enjoyed spending time with his aunt with her relaxed rules and fun demeanor. He was sure he was about to get a second night.

That Sunday in church, Tyler felt that the sermon seemed to be tailored directly toward him, and what he was embarking on with his golf journey. The text the pastor used came from a combination of 2 Timothy 1:7, "For the spirit God gave us does not make us timid, but gives us power, love, and self-discipline." And Philippians 4:13, "I can do all things through Christ who gives me strength." This message and these scriptures really resonated with Tyler and the excitement he was feeling for his newfound sport. It was as if God was encouraging him directly, by way of Reverend Brown.

After the service, as always, Tyler made his way to speak to Deacon Chapman to say hello. Deacon Chapman and his grandfather, Frank, had been good friends up until Frank passed away 6 years ago. They'd both attended high school together. As adults, they both worked as bus drivers for the local transit authority. They'd sang together in the church's male choirs, and had met for coffee a few times a week. They had been really good friends.

When Tyler was younger, Deacon Chapman would give him one dollar every Sunday. As he got older, Tyler no longer received dollars from Deacon Chapman, instead, he received good advice and words of encouragement. Tyler looked forward to sharing highlights about his week with Deacon Chapman in exchange for his warm grandfatherly smile, pat on the back, and encouraging words. Over the last few years, it also seemed as if his time with Deacon Chapman was in some way for him, a connection to his grandfather as well.

Today, when he saw Deacon Chapman, he told him about his new experience and first lesson with golf. This time, Deacon Chapman's warm smile was even bigger and brighter than normal. He said, "Tyler, that is great! Golf is a fun sport to play, and can be a great way to get to meet new people and make new friends. I look forward to you telling me what you learn and how your game progresses."

"I will and maybe you will get to come see me play one day."

"I would love to!"

Tyler then went over to his mom and dad to ask about spending the night at Aunt Asia's house.

"Can Chloe and I spend the night with Aunt Asia tonight, since tomorrow is a holiday? I already asked her, and she said she was okay with it if you both were."

Joy responded, "It's fine for you to stay, but you need to do some reading while you're there. I know it's not a school day, but it would be a great time to do some leisure reading on a topic of your choosing."

"Yes! Okay, that works for me!"

Tyler was agreeable to this since it was typical that he and Aunt Asia would read and discuss books together anyway. Happy to get to spend extra time with his aunt, Tyler ran over to his Aunt Asia to let her know the good news.

"My mom said we could stay as long as I do some reading tomorrow while I am there."

"That sounds good, and I know just the reading you should do."

"What's that?"

"You've found a new sport that you're really excited about, and I am excited for you to have this new experience. However, golf has a fascinating history that I think is important for you to understand while you're learning the game. So, I want you to do some research, and write a short essay on the history of golf."

"Okay. I have no idea what I'll find, but I am curious, and I am cool with writing an essay.

Before leaving church, Ronald talked to his friend, Deacon Chapman. During the conversation, Deacon Chapman said, "Ronnie, Tyler told me that he's started taking golf lessons. I told him that is great! I encouraged him to take his time, focus on his lessons, and have fun. Ronnie, golf is a great game and will open up a world of opportunity for him. Not enough young Black kids play, and they miss out on a fun sport that they could be great at and use to network with all kinds of people. Good for him, and good for you, opening him up to it. I didn't think you played the game. What made you introduce him to golf?"

"I don't play, and I didn't introduce him to the sport. His friend, Ryan, told him about the lessons. I was hoping Tyler would spend this off season focusing on his basketball game and spending more time at the shop. This golf stuff came out of nowhere."

"Ronnie, he's young. He should explore different things and have different experiences with education and sports. I know you loved basketball and you were very good at it. I also know you built that shop into what is it today and have done very well with that too. Still, you have to be open to the fact that Tyler may, or may not, be as in love with either of those things. And that will have to be ok."

Ronald, while not excited to think about Tyler not taking over the family business, focused in on the golf aspect. He said to Deacon Chapman, "I hear what you're saying, and while it pains me to think about Tyler not following in my footsteps, I have equal concern about what his experiences may be trying to play golf. You know better than I do the history of golf as it pertains to Black people, and not a whole lot has changed. What types of experiences or encounters might he have?"

"Yes, I do know how we have been treated, and excluded from the sport. Yes, he will most likely have some uncomfortable encounters along the way if he enjoys and excels at the game. However, you and Joy have done a great job of raising him to be an intelligent young man. He'll be equipped to handle any situation thrown at him and he will learn from them. Ronnie, there are plenty of examples of strong Black people that have dealt with the challenges and made breakthroughs in many different fields, courts, and board rooms, and they need for others to follow their lead. Once the door has been kicked open, we have to keep it open, and the only way to do that is to continue to flow energetic, talented, and qualified brothers and sisters through it. Think about some of the great Black trailblazers and those that followed. Venus and Serena Williams - Tennis, Art Shell – Coaching Football, Clifton Wharton (first Black CEO of a Fortune 500 company in 1987 at TIAA), and Ursula M. Burns (first Black woman to be a CEO of a Fortune 500 company Xerox). The door was kicked open for Tiger, then he left his mark on the game. Maybe it's time for Tyler to go make his mark in the sport. Tell Tyler, Deacon Chapman said, Go Fore It!"

Knowing what Deacon Chapman said had merit, Ronald, with an awkward feeling of awe and hesitation, then said, "Yes, Deacon Chapman, you make a valid point."

"Ronnie, I really would like to continue our conversation, but I have to run. Since tomorrow is a day off, how about you meet me at Carrie's Coffee Café tomorrow morning at 7:00? My treat." Ronald agreed and looked forward to continuing their conversation.

Coffee Talk

The next morning at 7:00am, Ronald met Deacon Chapman at Carrie's Coffee Café, which happened to be directly across the street from Ronald's automotive repair shop. Many of the café employees, including Carrie, the shop's namesake and owner, knew both gentlemen. Carrie came out and greeted both men as they took a seat in one of the café's corner booths. Ronald knew Carrie because he stopped in every morning to get his coffee before going across the street to start his day. He said hello to Carrie as she approached the table and attempted to introduce Deacon Chapman. Carrie cut him off, saying, "I know Chap, he's in here, in this very booth, every day, he and his buddies. They're in here shortly after you. They sit here having their coffee and breakfast, solving the issues of the world, and admiring your hard work and discipline running your business across the street."

Deacon Chapman smiled and said, "Hello, Carrie. I hope you are having a marvelous day on this beautiful Monday morning."

Carrie responded, "My day, as always, is off to a great start, and it will be better than yesterday." Carrie lived with the mindset that her best days were always ahead, never behind her.

Deacon Chapman responded, "I know that's right," with a warm gentlemanly smile.

Carrie gave a smile in return said, "I'll get you fellas a couple of coffees to get you started."

Ronald looked at Deacon Chapman and said, "I didn't know you're here every day. Do you really say that about me and the shop?"

Deacon Chapmen nodded and said, "Yes, I meet a few of the fellas here every morning and we start our day together. You occasionally come up. We are all proud of you. We remember when Joe owned that place, and you worked there. It was a decent shop. Joe and the fellas working there did a good job and were reliable. However, you have grown the shop greatly. The partnerships you have with the local businesses have helped create a steady stream of business for you, in addition to taking the time to service those of us with old fixer uppers needing small repairs. I will also tell you I am really proud of you for the partnership you have with the automotive tech school too.

You have helped a lot of young guys in this town gain invaluable experience and develop a trade that will allow them to earn an honest living. Many times, guys would not be so open, for fear of someone duplicating their business model, or taking something from them; you know, like a crabs in a barrel mentality. But your example has rubbed off on other business owners in this town. I've seen Tom, who owns the plumbing and HVAC company, hire from the tech school, as well as Jim, the electrician, and even the steel and ironworkers union has developed a partnership with the tech schools. Your example has helped provide opportunities for a lot of young people in our town. I think this is all a really good example of something different for our kids.

In today's education system, the focus is on helping kids get college ready. While college is an outstanding opportunity, it is not the only path, and not every student is a college student. There are plenty of certificates and trade programs that can lead to great careers, or entrepreneurship opportunities for kids coming out of high school. Programs in the medical field, careers in clean energy, CDL licensed drivers, and electricians, the list goes on. Look at what your automotive training has done for you and your family.

I understand your profession is going to be impacted with the shift to electric vehicles, but my guess is that you will adjust. Add a few charging stations, do more tire and brake work. You will learn and hire people that can repair the electronic components of these new cars and trucks. My point is, I think it's important to show kids there are additional paths other than college. A college education is great, and if a kid has that desire, they should have the opportunity to experience it, without cost being a barrier to entry. But, if that's not the kid's desire, they shouldn't feel lost, without options, or made to feel less than kids that choose college. Ronnie, this is all a very long-winded way of saying I am really happy for you and proud of you. I know Frank was too." Not expecting such an endorsement, Ronald thanked Deacon Chapman for the compliment and kind words.

At that time, Carrie returned with the two coffees. Ronald and Deacon Chapmen both thanked her. Deacon

Chapman said to Ronald, "I'm not sure if you have taken the time to have breakfast here or not, but the waffles are amazing!"

Ronald said, "I haven't had them before, so now sounds like a great time to do so. I'll have the waffles as well, with a side of bacon, please."

Carrie replied, "You will love them, 2 waffles and bacon coming right up." Both the men thanked Carrie as she walked away from the table.

Ronald told Deacon Chapman, "I've thought a lot about what you told me yesterday at church. You made some really good points, but I have to tell you, the troublesome history of golf was all I could think about as I was taking Tyler to that first lesson. To be honest, I've still been thinking about it."

"I understand the feelings you have," said Deacon Chapman. "As a Black man who has endured many different forms of disrespect and racism, both overt and covert, these experiences have shaped how I, and we as Black people, interact, and handle certain situations. It also explains the rush of emotions you felt taking Tyler to his lesson. Ronnie, each generation has its own challenges. Tyler's generation has to be willing to engage and take advantage of the opportunities that your dad and I fought for, and that your generation moved forward. The world is more open, and more accepting today than it once was, but there are unquestionably still challenges and progress to be made.

You have to raise him to persevere, while at the same time teaching him about his past, and how to carry himself when he encounters those that are stuck in the way things were. It is not easy, but it's the current phase of our struggle for equality that we've been fighting for years to try to achieve. Fredrick Douglas, Booker T. Washington, Ida B. Wells, and others have done great work to make this moment possible for Tyler. Frank prepared you, and you have prepared Tyler, for this."

Ronald, now with a chest full of pride from the uplifting conversation and getting to stand on the shoulders of the great individuals Deacon Chapman had just referenced, lovingly remembered the lessons from his own father, and simply said, "Yes, this is Tyler's moment."

Just then, Carrie returned with their breakfast. "Here it is gentlemen," Carrie said, as she approached the table. Two identical plates held two waffles, each with the heat still rising up from them, two strips of bacon, and fresh fruit. Each plate was picturesque. Both men thanked Carrie and admired the care with which each plate was prepared, and how appetizing they both looked. Carrie told the men to enjoy, and that she would be back shortly to refresh their coffees. Deacon Chapman said, "Carrie, you are the best," as she walked away.

As the men began to enjoy their meals, Deacon Chapman asked Ronald, "Do you have a financial advisor?"

"A financial advisor? No, I don't have one of those. I have a good person at my bank that I call when I have a need. That works well for me. I don't have a lot of money, certainly not enough for an advisor."

"I disagree. You know Frank and I both retired from the transit system. It was a good job, but not something we would get rich doing. It was enough to make an honest living and raise our families. About 8 years before I thought I was ready to retire, I was introduced to a financial advisor named Nate. I was like you and did not think I needed an advisor. I did not have enough money to require his services. I still met with him anyway. He reviewed my information, and told me with the path I was on, I would end up running out of money during retirement. I would have been forced to get at least a part-time job, just to make ends meet. He gave me some guidance, which I followed, and I could have retired in 6 years and still been comfortable, instead of retiring in 8 just to go back to work later.

My point is, far too often, we as Black people don't know the proper resources to allow us to be successful. Then, when we do learn about the resources, we often can't afford it, don't want to spend the money for it, or think we don't need it. Then there's my favorite, we look at the brother or sister who leverages those resources and say, "They're trying to be like the White folk" or "They're uppity." All of which are just flat out crazy! This type of thinking prevents us from getting ahead, and is what has led to the way you feel about Tyler playing golf. It is one of the reasons we progress so slowly as a people, compared to others."

Ronald, still processing the first part of his conversation with Deacon Chapman, was in awe of the perspective being shared with him and said, "Okay, Deacon Chapman, I'm listening. Are you suggesting I need to speak with an advisor?"

Deacon Chapman, now knowing he had Ronald's full attention said, "Ronnie, it's probably a good idea. You're doing well at the shop and Joy earns a good income. You need to review your retirement plans and how you're planning to set up Tyler and Chloe after you are gone.

"Yes, but I am setting it up for Tyler to take over the business after me, so that part is taken care of."

"I hear you, but there is a chance that Tyler will not want to take over the business. I know that being able to keep the business in the family is great for a legacy, but at what cost? It may be at the expense of Tyler's happiness, if his heart is not in it. An advisor can give you options for if you turn the business over to Tyler, or if you sell it. Now think about when you bought the business from Stallworth. You gave him a lump sum and paid him out over the next several years. You have hired a lot of young guys that would love to carry on your legacy, and would do a great job if Tyler doesn't want to. My point is, an advisor can help you and Joy make a plan that will work for what each of you wants to do, including retiring early enough to enjoy watching your children grow up."

"Deacon Chapman, this is a lot of information to take in over one breakfast. I'm glad we got to talk, now I have a lot to digest. I am smart enough to take good advice when it's given though. What is the name and number of your financial advisor?"

"My guy has retired from the business, but I will get a referral from him for you."

While still processing all that Deacon Chapman had just shared, and not fully accepting the idea of Tyler not carrying on the business, Ronald knew deep down that what Deacon Chapman said was true, and he needed to have a plan B in case Tyler did take a different direction. He also liked the idea of speaking with an advisor, knowing that it couldn't hurt, and he didn't know, what he didn't know. The two men enjoyed the rest of their breakfast, and soon parted ways to make the most of a Monday holiday.

Tyler's Essay

Similar to Ronald, Tyler and Chloe's morning started off with a nice hot breakfast too. Aunt Asia, knowing her niece and nephew well, started the morning off with Tyler's favorite, chocolate chip pancakes, 3 strips of bacon, and peach slices. Even Chloe enjoyed Aunt Asia's pancakes, although she enjoyed making a mess in the syrup as much as she loved eating the pancakes. All of which made Asia happy. She enjoyed seeing the smiles on her niece and nephew's faces. As they sat down at the table for breakfast, Tyler said, "Thank you Aunt Asia, for making our favorite pancakes for breakfast."

"You are very welcome, Nephew Tyler."

Reflecting back on their card game from the previous night, and with a smirk on his face, Tyler asked Asia, "Did you make my favorite breakfast today because you cheated at the game last night? I played a draw 10 on top of your draw 10, you should have gotten 20 cards."

Asia immediately responded, "No, remember we read the directions, and you cannot put a draw 10 on top of a draw 10. We have this conversation every time you want to play that game. Give me back my pancakes."

They both began to laugh as the banter went back and forth about who was right and who was wrong about the rules, and who really won the game. It was an epic conversation that took place after each of their card games. A conversation that Tyler appeared to enjoy having more than Asia, who refused to let him win at anything if she could help it. Tyler was known to talk big trash with the best of them when he was able to beat a family member at any card or board game. He was super competitive in that way and hated to lose.

After a few minutes of talking about the card game, Asia took the opportunity to change the topic of the conversation.

"Okay, enough of that. So, Tyler how long do you think your essay on the history of golf should be."

"I really don't know much about the history of golf, so I don't know how much information I'll find. It'll depend on how much material is available, and what direction I take the essay. Is there a certain length you think it should be?"

"Golf is a pretty big sport, so you should be able to find a lot of information on it to write a nice essay. I would say make it at least 500 words, but don't limit yourself. If you get excited about what you find, have at it. I know this is a day out of school for you, so I don't expect you to spend your entire day reading and writing. Spend a couple of hours on it this morning, and we can watch a movie or play a game this afternoon before I take you two back home."

"Okay, Aunt Asia, that sounds like a plan." After breakfast, he pulled out Asia's tablet and headed to her home office to begin his research.

While Tyler was working on his assignment, Asia and Chloe spent time doing learning actives as well. They read a few books, practiced colors, built with Legos, and Chloe's new favorite thing, taking apart Tyler's old toys. While Chloe entertained herself for a little while, Asia pulled out her tool kit to start putting together a small end table she'd picked up several days earlier. She liked this table because she could use it to display a few of Tyler's projects and cards he had given her, and it had a drawer that she could put Chloe's toys in. When Asia pulled out the tools and began to take the table parts out of the box, Chloe immediately walked over to the tool kit and pulled tools out.

Asia just laughed and said, "Do you know what to do with that screwdriver or that socket wrench?" Chloe simply looked up at Asia and smiled. Asia smiled back, and asked again jokingly, "Well, do you? Do you know what to do with those?" She continued to pull the parts of the table out of the box and began to read the directions for putting the table together. To Asia's surprise, the statement "easy to assemble" written on the side of the box was correct. The assembly only required 3 tools, and 30-45 minutes for one person to assemble. Relieved, Asia said, "Whew, this won't take me all day to do."

When she reached down to pick up her screwdriver, she noticed that Chloe had taken it over to one of her brother's remote-controlled cars and was in the process of unscrewing the spoiler from the back of the car. Asia said, "Girl, your brother will be upset with both of us. I guess you're telling me a 2-year-old does know what to do with a screwdriver. Come here and leave that car alone."

Chloe looked at Asia and said, "Car...car."

Asia told her, "Yes, it is a car, but you have to stop." Now, knowing that Chloe knew what to do with a screwdriver, she allowed her to help put the table together.

Again, to Asia's surprise, Chloe actually knew what she was doing. While she wasn't strong enough to tighten the screws, she could certainly help get them started. This process of letting Chloe help with the screws made the project take a little longer, but it sure made it more interesting and fun. Once the table was completed, Asia looked at Chloe and said, "Maybe your father should take you to the shop with him. You may want to take it over one day."

Chloe looked up at her aunt, smiled and said, "Yup."

Asia asked, "Do you like watching your dad fix things?"

Chloe replied, "Yes." Asia, not sure this 2-year-old really understood what she was saying, thought to herself, this girl might really want to work in the shop one day. I need to make sure Ronald pays attention to his daughter; it may be her that carries on the family business, not Tyler.

Remembering that Tyler was in the room working on his assignment, Asia said to Chloe, "Hey, let's go check on your brother." They walked over, well Asia walked and Chloe ran, to the room where Tyler was working. They leaned in to ask him, "Hey, Nephew Tyler, how is it going in there?"

"So far so good. I'm finding a lot of information about golf. How it possibly started in Scotland but people aren't really sure, and when it became popular in America. However, I am finding that in golf's early years, while many Black people worked at golf courses and were knowledgeable of the game, they were not allowed to play. In fact, a Black man, Dr. George Grant, invented the first golf tee, which is the one still used today, but at the time he invented it, he wasn't allowed to play on most golf courses. Golf was one of the last sports to fully integrate and allow Black men and women to compete against White men and women. Also, I'm not able to find much information about many recent Black players, other than Tiger Woods. I've found information about Charlie Sifford, and Lee Elder, who broke barriers in the PGA and at the Masters in August, and William "Bill" Powell, who was the first Black man to build his own public integrated golf course, but no other recent golfers. Aunt Asia, do you know of any Black players other than Tiger that I can look up?"

"Unfortunately, Tyler, I do not. I don't know a lot about golf, but you are correct that there have not been many Black people that have played professionally. How about this, look just a little bit more and if you're unable to find anyone, maybe you can write about that in your essay? Also, since you're doing so much digging and research, if you want, you can wait until next weekend to write your essay?"

"Thanks, Aunt Asia, but if it is okay, I want to keep working on this right now. I'm really interested in what I'm finding, so I want to dig a little more, and still write my essay today."

"That will be fine. Chloe and I will be in the living room watching a movie until you're done."

A couple of hours later, as Asia and Chloe were finishing up their second movie, Tyler came out of the office with his essay in hand. Chloe, having missed her brother over the last few hours, ran over to him. He picked her up and gave her a big hug as he walked over to take a seat on the couch next to his aunt. He handed Asia the essay and said, "I see why you wanted me to learn more about the history of golf. What I just read actually makes me a little angry, disappointed, and I guess somewhat confused. Why was this sport so delayed, and allowed to be so slow to integrate?

It was as recent as 1975 that a man at one of the tournament championship courses said, 'Golfers will be White, and the caddies will be Black.' What? In 1975, we still could only carry White people's bags? And just 30 years ago, in 1990, a private country club in the south allowed Jews, women, Lebanese, and Italians, but not Blacks. What?! But not Blacks, how could that be in this country in 1990? Oh, and wait, I read an article where a broadcaster said the younger White golfers would have to gang up on the Black golfer to beat him, and the other broadcaster, a White lady, said they would have to 'lynch him in a back alley.'

He was the best golfer in the world. Why wouldn't the sports broadcasters celebrate him, not want to kill him in such an evil way? Don't they know how horrible it is to talk about lynching a Black man, and the fear and anger it creates for Black people? Another person said they would invite him over for dinner and serve him fried chicken. What a stereotypical and racist statement! Why would he assume the best golfer in the world eats chicken? Just because he is Black? I guess I understand why I could not find many current Black golfers to study and write about. Do we really have the opportunity to be successful in this sport?"

Asia looked helplessly at her nephew, contrite for what he had just learned and wishing it was not so. She simply drew him near to her to embrace him and said, "All great questions. I wish I had answers for you, or could tell you that it wasn't as it seemed. But, the reality is that what you read is in fact, true. There were, and there still are, people out there that are not accepting of seeing Black people as being equal. They don't want to see Black people become members of their country clubs, play on their golf courses or be in their executive boardrooms. I know your dad has had conversations with you about how to carry yourself as a young Black man, and how some White people may view you. If you continue to play this sport, you are going to have to keep those lessons close. You will have to learn to overlook or ignore some of the things that people may say to or about you. I pray you never experience these types of things, but the reality is you probably will."

Tyler, with a look of youthful innocence and turmoil on his face, looked at his aunt and said, "Yes, I get it. I guess this feels different because the other conversations we had about slavery, the civil rights movement, and overall acts of discrimination, all seemed to be so long ago. Fifty or Sixty years ago, not 5 or 10 years ago. Not still happening today."

Tyler broke eye contact with his aunt and held his head in his hands. Moments later, he leaned up and looked at his sister, then at his aunt, with a certain gleam in his eye and thanked his aunt for giving him the assignment. He said, "I am a Black man like many before me. I am not an extraordinary person, but I am a person. There aren't many Black men that have had success in this game, for one reason or another, but I have an opportunity to change that. I am going to change that! Thanks to other trail-blazing Black male and female sports figures like Doug Williams, John Thompson, C. Vivian Stringer, Dawn Staley, and others, I get to stand on their shoulders and continue to change the narrative. I've been given the opportunity to learn to play this game, and I am going to help change what is possible."

Asia, somewhat taken aback by the tone in his voice and the fire in his eyes said, "That's right, Nephew. That is a choice you get to make, and you know I will support you however I can." Still astonished by the tone of his voice and the look in his eyes, Asia looked at Tyler, beaming with pride at the conviction shown by her nephew. This was something new to see from Tyler, but it wasn't new for Asia to see. She was used to seeing that same look in Ronald's eye when they were growing up and he was playing in big basketball games. When he bought his repair shop, and again when his children were born. She knew that Tyler had found his calling and his sport; he was going to make his impact.

Extended Family Dinner

With his mind racing around what he had just researched, the questions he still had, and the information his aunt shared with him, Tyler sat with Asia and Chloe to watch a movie together before Asia took them home for the evening. On the ride back, Asia could tell Tyler was still pondering what he had just experienced and learned, and what he was inspired to do. She engaged him in conversation asking, "So, Tyler do you have to get your own golf clubs, or a uniform?"

"They supplied clubs for me to use to get started, but I'll need to have my own soon. I'll need what is called 'proper golf attire' when I get to go on the actual golf course. I went to the pro shop, which is the place they sell golf clothes and some equipment, before we left practice. The prices of the golf stuff was really high. Hopefully, we'll be able to find it somewhere else a little less expensive. And, to be honest, I wasn't a fan of the clothes there, so I hope we can find better options too. All the pants were really expensive, and the shirts were either plain or had colors and patterns that I didn't like. There was nothing that really looked like me; nothing I would have been excited wearing."

"Stores like that will have limited options, and are in fact more expensive. I am sure your dad will be happy to take you to the sporting goods store to pick out the right set of golf clubs for you, and your mom and I will help you find some clothes you like. You have to like the clothes you're wearing. Like Deion Sanders says, 'If you look good, you feel good. If you feel good, you play good. If you play good, they pay good.' With an optimistic grin, Asia said, "Well you're not getting paid... yet. But you get the point."

Tyler also smiled, thinking about Asia's suggestion. He loved going to the sporting goods store with his dad, it was always an adventure for the two of them. They would go in for one thing and end up looking at everything else, like camping knives, fishing lures, boots, grilling supplies, and Tyler's favorite, the boats he hoped they would buy one day. After spending hours in the store, they would often forget what they went there for in the first place, and end up leaving with something totally different.

This would be the first time going to look for golf supplies, so there was no telling what they would leave with. He was also excited because both his mom and his Aunt Asia were fashionistas in their own right, and always fixed him up with nice, quality, pieces that looked good and felt good to the touch. This sounded like a brilliant plan to him and was something new he had to look forward to. It was also the perfect way to get him thinking about something other than what he had just researched for a little while.

A short drive later, Asia and the kids arrived at the house. They opened the door and were greeted by the warm inviting scent of a hearty home-cooked meal being prepared. Asia and the kids took in a deep breath, and in unison, she and Tyler said, "Wow, something smells good in here." Joy could be heard giggling in the kitchen and said, "Hey you guys are just in time for dinner; the food will be ready in a few minutes. Asia, you have to stay for dinner too. We're having Cornish hens, ham, wild rice, broccoli, and sweet potatoes, and I have already prepared enough for you. So, just come on in and relax." With an invitation or demand like that, how could Asia say no? So, she and the kids washed their hands and began setting the table, along with Ronald.

At the table after saying grace, Ronald asked, "How was everyone's day?"

Asia proudly shared, "Chloe and I put together my new table."

Ronald asked, "You and Chloe put it together?"

"Oh yes, your daughter is very helpful and is good with a screwdriver. You're going to need to start giving her some little projects to work on. She may be your next employee or co-owner."

Ronald looked at Asia, then Chloe and said, "You want to work at the shop?"

Chloe, with a twinkle in her eye and smile wide enough to brighten the already well-lit room, nodded her head and said, "Yes!"

Ronald smiled and said in a fairly condescending tone, "Ok."

Then Tyler spoke up and shared some of what he learned from his research on the game of golf. "I'm surprised at how recent it was that the game became widely available to Black people at the highest level, and how few Black people actually play at any level. I didn't understand the insensitive or racist comments that people have shared in the media. It just didn't make sense to me how this could be tolerated, excused, or even happen in today's times."

Ronald agreed and said, "It is inexcusable, and appalling that it still happens. Just think about the comments that were probably said directly to that handful of Black athletes on the golf course that weren't captured in the news or said on camera. Think about the blatant disrespect that was shown to them, or the uncomfortable situations they most likely faced in their travels to tournaments, in the locker rooms or going out for a meal. The world can be an ugly place, and golf has had no problems putting its ugly on display. I believe as Black people, as Black men, we have enough challenges and difficult situations all around us, why purposefully go where we are clearly not wanted, and deal with additional challenges?"

Tyler momentarily stopped eating and looked at his dad with a long thoughtful look on his face. He said in a confident and determined voice, "Because we have to. If we don't do something, if we don't try, then we don't know what we are missing out on, and they win. Then we don't make progress. If we don't continue to make progress, then the work of Bill Spiller, Charlie Sifford, Lee Elder, Tiger Woods, and Harold Varner III is lost."

Ronald, now at a rare loss for words, looked towards his son lovingly, proud, and in awe. Joy, surprised to hear her son speak with such passion and conviction in his voice, also beamed with pride as she too began to smile. She told her son, "I am so proud of you and your level of maturity and conviction in this decision." With a joyful smile on her face, Joy then told Tyler, "Now enjoy your meal because you are going to need your physical and mental strength, as well as your faith, to shield yourself from the fiery arrow that may someday be thrown your way."

Tyler looked at his parents and said, "Thank you for signing me up for the lessons. I'm inspired to do my best with golf, and to make a difference."

Joy told him again, "I'm proud of you, and I know your best will be good enough. I am glad your aunt had you do this research because it helped you learn on your own, what we would have struggled to explain to you. This is clearly something you want, and for that reason, we want it for you too. But it will be imperative that you always tell us about your experiences. The positive, exciting ones, and the uncomfortable ones that you may not fully understand. That will be the only way we can help and support you, or limit the impact a situation may have on you."

"Yes Mom, you know I will."

Ronald added, "Yes Tyler, open communication with your mother and me is a must. Also, I didn't get to tell you before, but on Sunday at church when I was talking to Deacon Chapman about you learning golf, he told me to tell you to Go Fore it! F.O.R.E."

Tyler laughed and said, "Hey, that's a golf term."

Everyone laughed and said, "Yes it is," with Ronald adding, "I hope you don't find yourself yelling that too often when you start playing on the golf course."

Asia then asked Tyler, "What about basketball?"

Ronald with an inquisitive look on his face, looked at Asia, then at Tyler, and asked, "What do you mean what about basketball?"

Tyler looked at Asia, then at his dad, and told him, "I am not really that into basketball. I mean, I like to play basketball, and I love when we spend time in the driveway playing, but I just don't enjoy all the practice and hard work required to be great at it. Basketball isn't enjoyable to me. It just feels like work."

A somewhat disappointed Ronald looked at his son and asked, "Are you sure?" Although, deep in his heart of hearts he already knew the answer. He could tell this last season on the court that Tyler did not seem to love what he was doing. That coupled with how quickly he took to golf after the season was over.

Tyler replied, "Yes I'm sure, but I don't want to disappoint you, and I still want to be able to play driveway pickup games with you."

"Son, you couldn't disappoint me for something you did or did not want to do. I want you to be happy. I love playing basketball. Basketball was and is my passion. Of course, I would love to share that with you, but it has to be what you want, not just because I want it for you."

Tyler, relieved that the conversation went so much better than he thought it might, looked lovingly at his dad and said, "Thank you, dad."

"The exception would be that you would still be working at the shop. I still need you to come help out because it would be great learning experience for you, even if you decide not to take it over one day." After having his breakfast conversation with Deacon Chapman, Ronald was starting to accept the fact that someday Tyler might tell him he wasn't interested in running an automotive repair shop. However, as he explained to Tyler, "The lessons you learn working at the shop about leadership, managing people, running payroll, and pride in your work, will be very helpful to you as you become your own man, and make your own living. In addition, learning to work on cars in this environment is invaluable. When I started, cars were simple, and almost anyone could work on them.

The cars today are much more complex. I continually take classes, and send my guys to take classes, to learn how to work on them. Moreover, there is a big shift to electric powered cars instead of gasoline. One of the major car companies has already said they will stop making gasoline-powered vehicles by the year 2035.

I've already made job offers to 2 guys to start next year when they graduate the tech program at Auto Tech College. They're taking concentrated classes on electric and hydrogen powered vehicles.

I need them in the shop now so we can start attracting these new customers, and all of us can stay ahead of the technology curve. I need them to help me convert a few of the garage bays into what they'll need for electric car servicing, and set up new electric charging stations The automotive servicing and repair business is going through a huge transition, and there won't be space for untrained mechanics. Having knowledge of it can serve as a way for you to earn a living, or save you money on your own servicing and repairs."

Tyler understood and said, "I'll continue to spend time and learn as much as I can at the shop. I'm not sure if that's the career path I want, but for now, I enjoy the extra time with you. I know it won't hurt to learn these additional life lessons, and learn the automotive trade through first-hand experience."

Asia then said to Joy, "I told Tyler that he and his dad can go together to find golf clubs, but you and I can help him find some nice threads. He said the clothes at the golf store were expensive, and he didn't like any of them."

Joy, always ready to go shopping said, "I have never shopped for golf clothes before, so this will be fun. First, we have to check the buy black for life group page for any black-owned shops. I've been more consciously supporting black-owned businesses when I can. I've found some nice companies on their site that I did not know existed."

Ronald, always ready to hit the sporting goods store, perked up as well. He said, "Yes I need to head over there this week anyway. I need some more wood chips for the smoker. I've always walked through the golf section but never actually stopped or looked at anything, so this is going to be an adventure. We can go tomorrow after you get out of school, so you'll have them for practice on Wednesday."

Tyler liked that idea saying, "Perfect, that sounds like a plan to me. I like hitting the sporting goods store."

Joy then told Asia, "I'm off until Wednesday, so you let me know when you want to hit the stores. I'll check the website tonight and tomorrow to see what I can find, so I'll be good to go tomorrow afternoon."

"Tomorrow afternoon works for me too." Asia then told Joy, "But girl, you put your foot in this dinner today! These hens are bangin', and these potatoes are on point. I might need to stay here tonight to sleep this off, and we can just go shopping when I wake up." The table erupted in laughter, and in agreement that Joy had made a terrific meal.

Meeting Coach Jackson

The next day, as promised, Ronald picked Tyler up after school, and they headed to the sporting goods store. On the drive, Ronald asked Tyler how his day was.

"It was good."

"What was good about it, did anything special happen?"

"Nothing special, it was a regular day. I did get to talk to Ryan at lunch about golf. I told him about what I learned looking up the history, and how surprised I was. He told me that he had never read up on the history but hearing me tell him about what I read made him understand the responses he gets when he tells people that he plays golf."

"What type of responses does he get?"

"He said people generally seem surprised. He said in a weird tone, people say things like, 'Oh really, what made you start playing?' or 'Oh well, are you any good?', 'Who taught you?' and 'Where do you get to play?' I mean, I guess it might not be racist, but it's almost as if they don't expect he should be able or allowed to play. I wonder if they respond to all kids that way or just the Black ones."

"Tyler that could be a form of overt racism. Meaning they are not being direct with their intent, but the underlining tone is condescending and rooted in racism and classism. It's the kind of actions that I want you to be able to recognize, so you can understand that person's true character. These are some of the types of fiery darts and arrows your mother was referring to at dinner last night, that you will have to shield yourself from and not overly react to.

People like that take for granted that you won't recognize their intent, or that you will respond in a demonstratively negative way. So demonstrative and so negative that they will use it as proof to illustrate why you don't belong in their clubs, on their golf courses, in their schools or in certain leadership or executive levels within corporate organizations. Do you understand what I am saying to you?"

"Yes, I understand. It is not right that it happens, but I understand."

"You are correct, it's not right. It really isn't right, but it clearly does happen. Did Ryan say that he has told his parents about his experiences?"

"I didn't ask."

"I'll mention it to Mark, because it's important that he knows and is able to support Ryan. Son, thank you for telling me about your lunch conversation with Ryan. This is the kind of good communication we have to be able to have."

When they arrived at the sporting goods store they headed over to the grilling section first to pick up the wood chips that Ronald needed for his smoker. While in the grilling section they ran into Coach Jackson, Tyler's new golf coach. He recognized Tyler and said, "Hey, Tyler right?"

"Yes, and this is my dad."

Coach Jackson then turned to Ronald and said, "Hello I'm Jack; the kids call me Coach Jackson."

"Hello, nice to meet you. I saw you giving the lesson on Saturday. I didn't get to introduce myself with all of the parents and kids there, but it's a pleasure to meet you. Also, thank you for sharing your time with the kids. I know Tyler really enjoyed the lesson and is fired up about playing golf. In fact, we're in here tonight to find him some clubs. If you have some time, maybe you can help us out, I really don't know the first thing about golf or buying golf clubs."

"Sure, I have some time. I would love to help the two of you pick out some clubs. It's my pleasure teaching the kids the game. It was hard for me to believe Tyler had never picked up a club before, he was a natural. Really smooth and confident swing, keeps his head down, and his shoulders square. He will have to work on not trying to kill the ball, and keeping his club face more closed, but he can fix those things pretty easily."

"Thank you for the help because you just confirmed that I don't know anything about this game; head down, face open, kill the ball, all a foreign language to me." His comment made everyone laugh. Ronald then asked Coach Jackson, "So how did you, a young Black man, I assume in your 30s or 40s get involved in golf, and even to the point that you're able to coach the kids?"

Coach Jackson, with a smile on his face, told Ronald, "I'm 36. I started playing golf as a young boy. I grew up near a semi-private golf course in my hometown. Golf is a big deal there. A lot of people come down from up North during the winter months to escape the bitter cold, and they play some golf. My dad would caddie through the winter to earn a little extra cash. When I got old enough, I worked on the grounds crew, mowing the fairways and tending to the bunkers. At certain times during the summer months, which was the slow season, they would let us play the course.

Being a caddie, my dad knew the course extremely well and what clubs to use when. To be completely honest, he knew how to use the clubs better than many of the golfers he would caddie for. But you know how it goes. Anyway, being at the course so often, he had regulars that he would caddie for, and as they would buy new clubs, bags, and other equipment, they would give him the old ones. He would bring that equipment home, clean it up, and soon he had a complete set of clubs, including a bag, that he gave to me as my first set of clubs. Mismatched as could be, but they served their purpose. I would go out in the backyard and take practice swings for hours. I spent weekends at the range hitting practice balls, and when allowed, I played the course.

I enjoyed the game and before long, I got pretty good at it. I wanted to play on the high school team, but in my town, you had to pay to play sports. For golf, you had to pay to be on the team, pay for your entry to the tournaments, and buy your own equipment and attire. My family didn't have money for all of that, so I couldn't play for the school. However, the cool part of my golf journey was earning my college scholarship. By my senior year in high school, my dad had been coaching me, and I'd been practicing hard and getting on the course as much as I could. My game had gotten pretty good. So, I saved up my money to pay my entry fee as an independent player for one of the regional tournaments that came to town.

I played some of my best golf that day and placed 4th, which was good enough to get invited to play in an invitation-only tournament the following month. I placed well enough in that one to be invited to another and another. The last tournament I made it to, the winner received a scholarship to the state university to play golf. And guess where the tournament was played? My home course! I played extremely well in that tournament. Although I didn't win the tournament and get that scholarship, my play caught the attention of a scout for an out-of-state Historically Black College. My grades, combined with my golf performance, earned me a partial academic and partial athletic scholarship. Meaning that neither me, nor my parents had to take out loans for me to go to college.

Ronald said, "Man that is a heck of a story. Did you have a chance to go pro, or get on the amateur tour?"

"I believe I was good enough, but it's not just about being good. You need sponsors and that is easier said than done for us. However, I got more from the game than I ever expected; the college experience, a great education, a good job, and getting to help kids by teaching them the game of golf.

When I was a young man, I could remember my dad telling me about Charlie Sifford, and his perseverance and tenacity to win the United Golf Association National Negro Open 6 times. I can just imagine the drive and fire he had to have in his belly to get the PGA to remove the "Caucasian-only" clause. To be the type of person that someone like Jackie Robinson would publicly endorse to receive his tour card, and to deal with the overt racism he had to endure to make it possible for me to enjoy this game. How could I not make the most of my opportunity? How could I not give back to kids like Tyler who will get to make their own mark on the game and the world as well? Ronald, I am blessed!"

Ronald and Tyler both just smiled and nodded their heads. At that time, Coach Jackson said, "Here we are, these are the clubs I recommend you get. It's a full set of clubs, which will allow you to get a feel for swinging your driver, woods, and irons. Also, they are fairly inexpensive so you won't have to feel bad about moving on from them in a few years when you've outgrown them."

Tyler said, "That makes sense, and they look cool."

Coach Jackson said, "Yes, and they look cool," as he chuckled. He then told Tyler and Ronald, "I have to run, but don't forget to pick up a pair of golf shoes too, they'll come in handy for you when you head to the golf course soon. Tyler, I will see you tomorrow at practice. Ronald, it was a pleasure meeting and talking to you."

Ronald said, "Likewise Coach, we'll see you tomorrow." Ronald and Tyler picked up the clubs, found some shoes, and headed to pay for them, then to the car.

Now We Are Golfing

The next day, with Joy still being off from work, she decided that she would pick Tyler up from school and take him to his golf lesson. By now, she had seen and heard Tyler's excitement about golf. She'd had a conversation with Ronald about his feelings, and Ronald had told her about meeting Coach Jackson while out buying the clubs. Now it was time for her to experience this excitement for herself. When Joy picked Tyler up, as was the norm, she asked him how his day was, and as usual, he responded, "It was good." Which caused Joy to ask a follow-up question. "What happened today that stands out to you?"

"We had to do the school's physical fitness test today in P.E., and I did really well. I hit all of the targets, plus 13 on the seated V, 45 sit-ups in a minute, and 15 pull-ups. I wasn't the best in my class, but I did do really well. I was excited and proud of myself."

"Oh, Tyler that is great! I didn't know you were doing that testing today. Had you been practicing for it?"

"No, well not really. I forgot until last week that it was coming up. I missed hitting the sit-up goal last year, and I did want to improve on that. So, I started practicing my sit ups last week. I'm not really sure that made a big difference, but it felt good getting to hit the goal this year."

"Tyler, I am very proud of you. You set a goal and achieved it. Now are you ready for your golf lesson today?"

"Thank you, Mom. Oh yes! I am ready for golf today. Do you have my golf clubs in the back"?

"I sure do. I'm looking forward to seeing you hit a few balls today," Joy said as she turned and looked at Tyler with a warm motherly smile.

Shortly after, they pulled up to the driving range. Joy let Tyler out of the car to go meet up with Ryan, who was already there, while she went to find a parking spot. Once parked, Joy walked through the Pro Shop on the way out to the range. While inside, she looked around at the equipment and the golf clothes that were on display. She quickly saw what Tyler was referring to about the clothes. Nothing in the store stood out to her. The colors and patterns on the shirts were nothing special; no pop of color, no character, and certainly all overpriced. While she had only found a handful of options on the buy black for life group page, she liked what she saw there more than what the pro shop had to offer. She thought it would be nice if there were more Black clothiers involved in creating clothes for the Black golfer. That would certainly help with getting more of our children interested in wearing the clothes and learning the game. She tucked that thought away in her mind for later.

Joy headed out to the driving range and looked for the seating area Ronald had mentioned to her, which she easily found down the walkway and on the left. As she approached, she saw a handful of other parents already seated. She walked over, nodded, waved, and said hello to the other parents already there. As she took her seat, she took note of the other parents, the children on the range, the instructors, how nice the facility was, and all the diversity. Joy exhaled slightly, as a look of peace and delight came to her face. Joy had a true appreciation for the fact that she and Ronald were raising a well-rounded young man. A person who was willing to experience new things on his own and develop his own opinions about what he experiences. A young man who was comfortable being authentically himself in all of his interactions.

Tyler, Ryan, and Coach Jackson were working together in stalls 5 and 6. Today the focus was on using their irons. The proper way to swing them, the distances they could expect to hit the ball with each one, and the difference in swinging them from the tee box. Both Tyler and Ryan were hitting the ball well today. Coach Jackson was impressed with Tyler's progress, and more than once called him a natural. Even Ryan said to him, "Tyler, you're killing the ball." Tyler truly was dialed in on the ball. Due to playing other sports, his focus on technique and natural athletic ability was clearly shining through. He was extremely coachable, practiced good mechanics, and had a desire to be successful.

Coach Jackson said, "Tyler, I'm taking Ryan back out to the golf course on Saturday afternoon and we have room for one more, do you think you and your dad will be able to come too?"

"I am sure of it. I've been looking forward to going out on a real golf course. Do you think I'm ready?"

Coach Jackson said, "Yes you're hitting the ball well. There will always be something new to work on or learn, but you have the basics and you can continue to learn on the course."

"Tyler, that will be great. We're going to be golf buddies even sooner than we thought!," exclaimed Ryan.

"Yes, golf buddies! Thank you, Coach Jackson. I'm already looking forward to Saturday!"

The three continued the lessons, which concluded with 15 minutes on the putting green. After the lesson ended, Tyler ran over to his mom to share the great news.

"Mom! Mom! Coach Jackson says I can go with him to the golf course this Saturday. Ryan and I are already going to be golf buddies."

"That is exciting, Tyler! I saw you hitting the balls, you looked really good out there. I'm sure you will do well on the golf course."

"Yes, I felt good too. I still have a lot to work on but I'm happy with my progress so far, and really happy to be going to the golf course on Saturday. Mom, would it be okay if I get up an hour early every morning to go in the backyard and hit practice balls?"

"You, who doesn't like to get up on time as it is? You want to get up an hour early to practice your golf game?"

"Yes, I want to be ready on Saturday."

"Well, alright. As long as you set your alarm, and you're ready for school on time, you can get up early to practice. I just still can't believe you want to get up early."

"Thanks, Mom. I really like the feeling of hitting the ball, and I'm ready to learn how to hit the ball with even more precision."

Thursday and Friday morning, to his mother and father's surprise, Tyler did in fact get up an hour early on his own to practice his swing. He went outside while the dew was still fresh on the grass and the birds just starting to sing. Tyler sat his golf bag right by the back door, as he sat down and began to put his new golf shoes on. He wanted to get used to wearing them, and how they felt on his feet, before wearing them on the golf course. He walked around and did a few stretches to get his blood flowing and his heart rate up. Once good and loose, he pulled his pitching wedge out of the bag and began to take a few practice swings without hitting a ball.

Once he felt good about that, he pulled a couple of handfuls of plastic practice balls from his bag. He hit 10 to 15 with his wedge, then switched to his 7 iron to hit another set, followed by another couple of sets with his hybrid, 3 wood, and driver. If he had additional time, he would spend it hitting balls with his driver. That was the club that gave him the most trouble, and he wanted to get better with it. Tyler was feeling more and more confident with each club, with each swing. By the end of his practice on Friday morning, he was not only looking forward to Saturday's trip to the golf course, he was looking forward to seeing how well he could do.

Saturday

Even though he had practice on Saturday morning, Tyler still got up early and hit his normal 75 to 100 practice balls, before taking his shower and having breakfast. That morning at breakfast, Ronald said to Tyler, "Son, I have to say, I'm impressed you've been so diligent about your golf practice. You've gone from a person that will hit the snooze button 5 times, and wait to get pulled out of the bed, to now getting up an hour early to practice. I would have never imagined you would do that."

Tyler smiled and said, "I really like golf, and I'm going to be great at it. You've always told me that in order for me to be good at anything, I have to put in the hard work, and I have to have grit. So, I'm putting in the work."

"You're right. I have told you that, and it is true. I used to do the same thing with basketball. I would be in the gym early for conditioning before practice, and would stay late to practice my free throws and watch film. I understand your grind and that feeling you have right now. I love that you've found something you enjoy and you have such discipline with it."

"Not only does it feel good swinging the golf club, but I feel more confident in other things too."

"Really, like how? Give me an example."

"Well, now that I'm getting up earlier, and practicing before taking my shower and heading out to catch the bus, I'm feeling more awake and alert in homeroom. Also, in science lab yesterday, we did a group experiment, and we had to have someone debrief it for our group. Normally, I would shy away from speaking to the class, and let one of the other group members do the presentation. Yesterday, I volunteered to present. I knew the material, and I had confidence in myself being able to speak about it intelligently to the class. Mrs. McLamb said I did a great job, and we got an "A" on the lab work."

"Wow, that is great, Son. I guess golf is a pretty good influence on you, because I know you definitely didn't like speaking in front of a group before. Good for you! Well, come on, let's get out of here so you're not late for your lesson. Remember, we have to drop your sister off with your Aunt Asia on the way."

Tyler finished up his breakfast and they headed out the door. Fortunately, Asia's house was on the way to the range, so it wasn't out of the way. When they pulled up, Asia came out to the car to get Chloe, so Tyler and Ronald could continue on to the range.

"Hey, guys! Tyler, check you out, you're looking good in your new golf clothes. Do you like them?"

"Yes, they feel good. Thank you for going shopping with Mom."

"You are welcome. Have fun and good luck!"

"Thank you."

A few short minutes later, they were at the range. They arrived early, so Tyler stayed in the car while Ronald found a parking spot and together, they walked to the range. This time, the walk was a little different for Ronald than the last time. He was no longer focused on the past. He knew Tyler was no longer naïve about the cruel history of the sport and was learning how to carry himself if faced with opposition. This time, the walk and Ronald's focus were on the beautiful, warm, sunny day the Lord had made, and getting to be a part of his son's first golf experience. Yes, for Ronald, today was a good day.

As Ronald and Tyler approached the range, they saw Coach Jackson standing near the stalls reading his clipboard.

"Hey Coach Jackson, good to see you again," Ronald said.

"Hello Ronald, what's going on Tyler? Tyler are you ready to hit some balls, and play the course today?"

"Yes! I've already been up hitting a few practice balls this morning. I am ready."

"Coach, he has been getting up early before school to hit balls. I have never seen him up early on his own for anything. He's looking forward to this." Ronald added.

"Tyler, that is awesome. I love that discipline. Keep that up, I might be watching your highlights on ESPN one day."

"That's the plan, Coach!" exclaimed Tyler.

Tyler and Coach Jackson headed over to a stall to begin warming up, while Ronald headed to the seating area. A short time later, Ryan met Tyler at the neighboring stall, and Ryan's dad, Mark, took a seat beside Ronald. Mark and Ronald engaged in some small talk about the weather, work, and sports. Ronald then discussed the conversation he and Tyler had about covert and overt racism, and the comments that Ryan had shared with Tyler. He also told Mark about the research and essay that Tyler had done on the history of golf. He said the essay really helped to do the heavy lifting for helping Tyler to understand the history, and the situations he might encounter in the sport. Mark was very appreciative of the conversation and the insight. He mentioned that he and Ryan's mother, Courtney had discussed whether or not to share their thoughts about the game, and how that would impact Ryan's view. However, having him do his own research and form his own opinion sounded like a much better idea.

Moments later, the boys came over to gather their dads, to head to the golf course. Both boys were very excited. They'd had a great session on the range and were ready to take their talents to the course. The four of them headed over to the area where the golf carts were parked. Tyler and Ronald loaded Tyler's clubs onto the first cart, while Ryan and Mark loaded Ryan's clubs onto the second cart. They were joined by two other kids in their own cart, as well as Coach Jackson and Coach Donna. From the range to the first hole of the nine-hole course, it was a half mile cart ride down a gravel trail. As they rode down the trail, Ronald asked Tyler, "Are you excited? Are you ready?"

Tyler responded, "Absolutely! I've been thinking about this, and preparing for it all week. Now it's here." Ronald said, "Yes it's here, and it is a beautiful day for it too."

The four carts continued down the winding path. Tyler and his dad both took in the moment and enjoyed the scenery along the way. They noticed the birds singing in the trees, the squirrels running along the path, two Blue Jays sitting in a tree, and they passed a few deer standing in the distance. It was, in fact, a beautiful day to be outside in nature, and perfect for playing a round of golf. After a few minutes, the group pulled up to the welcome sign that read, "Welcome to Main Street Par 3 Executive Course." Ronald stopped the cart to document the moment by taking a picture with his son in front of the sign. Coach Jackson, riding in the cart behind Ronald and Tyler, stopped and got out to take the picture for them. "Yes, that's a good one. A great father and son picture. You'll have to frame that one," said Coach Jackson. Both Ronald and Tyler smiled and replied with a warm, "Thank you, Coach."

From there, hole number one was just a couple hundred yards away. As they approached the first tee box and exited the cart, both Tyler and Ronald were in awe at the beauty of the course. The first thing they noticed was the perfectly manicured green grass, and the change of the color from the middle of the fairway to the rough, along with the picturesque slope of the landscape. There were the tall pine trees and strong oaks that lined both sides of the fairway, from the tee box to the green. They took a deep breath and noticed the smell of the fresh cut grass mixed with the stream of running water of the creek behind them.

It was so serene they could taste the crisp clean air all around them. In the silence, they could hear the whispers of the afternoon breeze through the budding tree leaves, and the colorful spring flowers. They took a few steps and noticed the cloud-like feel of the soft grass beneath their feet. Within moments, father and son, had experienced the golf course with all five senses, and for different reasons were very happy to be there, doing it together.

Once everyone was out of their carts, Coach Jackson gathered everyone together to give some instructions on how the afternoon would be played.

"Okay everyone, we're here. Lisa, Derrick, and Ryan, you all have been here before. You know each other, and how we play the course. Tyler, congratulations on making your first trip to play the course. I know you know Ryan already. Also with us is Lisa, it's her 6th time on the course, and this is Derrick, who's playing for his 3rd time on the course. I have with me Coach Donna, who will help with instruction today. When we're on the golf course, it's an extension of your lesson on the range. We will be respectful of the other golfers, both in our group and others we encounter. You can keep your own score if you want, but our goal here is for instruction. We'll take a few redo shots, or mulligans as they're called, for you to get a feel for hitting certain shots, and in some cases, we'll just pick the ball up and move it. As I said, the goal is for you to learn and be encouraged, not discouraged. Be safe, be respectful of each other, learn from each other and have fun. Is everybody ready?

In unison, the group said, "Yes, Coach Jackson."

Coach Jackson said, "Lisa, how about you lead us off. Derrick, you next, followed by Ryan, then Tyler."

Lisa began putting on her glove as she walked back to her cart to get her club. When she got to the cart, she took a glance up at the tee box sign to read the distance to the hole. It was a 120-yard par 3. For this shot, she decided to use her 7 iron, which she pulled from her bag. Lisa walked up to the tee box and placed her ball on the tee. She looked down the fairway at the flag to notice the direction and intensity of the wind. It was just a light breeze blowing from right to left, not enough to truly alter her shot. She took a couple of steps backward to take a few practice swings.

When she was ready, Lisa stepped up to the ball and addressed it with her club. She took one more look at the flag, then her eyes were back on the ball. She took a controlled breath, in and back out, and began her back stroke. In one very smooth controlled motion, Lisa went into her back stroke, and swung through the ball very confidently and cleanly. Ping! And away the ball went, sailing through the clear blue sky and landing just feet to the right side of the green. "Great shot," shouted Coach Jackson and Coach Donna. The rest of the group added their own encouraging words to Lisa for her opening shot, to which Lisa smiled and said, "Thank you."

Next up was Derrick. After a similar process before hitting the ball, Derrick had his first shot land in the trees on the left side of the fairway. Coach Jackson said, "That's okay, you dropped your front shoulder. Tee up another ball and try it again. Derrick did tee up a second ball and this time, hit it much better; however, the ball landed in the sand bunker to the right of the green. Coach Jackson and Coach Donna both told him much better ball, but now he would get to work on his bunker game.

Next, Ryan stepped up to the tee box to take his shot. He placed his ball on the tee, and with a big swing, he sent his ball into flight. Again, everyone watched as a golf ball sailed across the open blue sky, before landing in the middle of the fairway. Coach Donna told Ryan, "Nice swing, you just hit under the ball, sending it almost straight up into the air. You're about 50 yards away from the green, which is the area surrounding the hole, but you're fine."

Last, it was Tyler's turn to hit his first golf ball on the golf course. He already had his glove on, and his 8 iron in his hand. Tyler put the ball on the tee, and like Lisa, took a couple of steps back to take a few practice swings. He looked at the flag, back at his dad, stepped up to the ball, and took one more look down the fairway at the flag. He took a breath and took his swing. Ping! The ball was in the air. Tyler knew the shot felt good, but as he looked, he couldn't spot the ball in the air. Ronald did see the ball and was full of pride watching his son's first golf ball streak across the sky on such a beautiful golf course. Then, after a few seconds that felt like minutes for Tyler, plop, the ball landed on the green about 30 feet from the hole. Tyler had hit an amazing first shot. The entire group cheered and congratulated Tyler on his tee shot.

The group all got back in their respective carts, and headed down the fairway to find their balls and complete the hole. Since Tyler's ball was already on the green, he needed to wait for the others to get their balls on the green as well. Ryan was the first to take his second shot. With one smooth swing he popped his ball right onto the front of the green. Derrick was next with his chip shot, which he beautifully popped onto the green as well. Lisa, on her second shot, got the ball within inches of the hole and was allowed to go ahead and tap it in for par, to which she received a round of applause. Next, Tyler took his second shot which ended up almost rolling off the green.

Coach Jackson told him, "Tyler, that was just a little too hard. You're okay. Take your time and try it again after Ryan and Derrick take their shots." Next, was Ryan's turn. His third shot rolled to within a foot of the hole, and a fourth shot landed him in the cup. "Nice job, Ryan," said Tyler and the rest of the group. Next, Derrick was up to take his third shot. He putted the ball, and it took a smooth slow roll to the hole. Just as it rolled closer to the hole, it got slower and appeared to stop moments before dropping in. "Great job, Derrick! Great putt!," yelled Coach Jackson and Coach Donna. Now it was Tyler's turn again. He walked up to the ball, and was careful not to hit it too hard again. However, this time he hit it a little too soft, and the ball didn't make it to the hole. Coach Donna told him, "It's okay, take your time."

Tyler approached the ball and hit it again. This time, with the right speed and power, but the ball stopped just inches to the right of the hole. From there he was able to knock it in. Tyler was excited to see the ball go in the hole. He knew it was two strokes over par, which was called a double bogie, but it was his first double bogie on a real golf course. He was now starting to understand the value of his continued practicing, especially his putting. Meanwhile, the rest of the group, and no one more than his dad, was applauding and cheering him on for successfully completing his first hole of golf.

Everyone got back in their respective carts, and began riding to hole number two. Ronald told Tyler, "Really nice start, Son. Not bad at all for your first time. It was beautiful watching that ball cutting through the afternoon sky!"

"Thanks, Dad. I didn't get to see it, I just heard it hit the ground. I have to keep working on my putting so next time I can get par."

A few short moments later, they pulled up to the second hole. Once everyone exited the carts, Coach Jackson gave some instruction, and suggestions for club choices. Each of the golfers then took their turn from the tee box, and finishing up the hole. This process continued for the remaining 7 holes they played that day. It was a great day for the young golfers, including Tyler, and his dad.

"Tyler, really nice first day on the course today. If I didn't know, I wouldn't have known this was your first time. How do you feel?," asked Coach Donna.

"I feel really good. It was fun. I certainly have a lot more work to do, but it was a great experience for sure. I know par for the course was 27, and I had at least 51 plus the lost balls that I'm not sure how to score. But, now I have a benchmark to work from."

Coach Donna said, "That is a great way of looking at it. Like Coach Jackson said, we aren't worried about the score here today; this is an extension of your learning. But I understand you wanting to have a benchmark."

Coach Jackson added, "Tyler it was your first experience on a golf course, and overall, it was a good one. Like many new golfers, it's difficult to be consistent with every stroke, and it's not like hitting balls at the range in ideal conditions. On the golf course, you have different length holes, bunkers, trees, and water hazards to navigate. All of which makes the game fun and challenging at the same time. Continue coming to your lessons, getting on the golf course, and your early morning practices, all with the intent of getting better every day. You do that, and you will have a terrific opportunity to be the great golfer you want to be."

"Thank you, Coach Jackson and Coach Donna. I will keep practicing, and I look forward to the next time," Tyler said to his Coaches.

"See you Monday at lunch golf buddy," Tyler then said to Ryan.

"Haha, See you at lunch golf buddy. And good job today Tyler," Ryan said in return.

Ronald then thanked the coaches for their time, and for creating this experience for the kids. He also said so long to Mark, as he and Tyler got in their cart to drive back up to the car. On the ride up the path, Ronald turned to his son and said, "Tyler, nice job out there today. You found something that you liked, and you took the initiative to do the work necessary to learn it and excel. I was really proud watching you play today. Something I don't know how to do, and that I couldn't do when I was your age. You are your own person, and creating your own moments. I am very proud of you, Son."

"Thank you, Dad. I'm really glad you were able to come. It was great having you there with me today, just like at all of my basketball games."

Low Country Boil

When they got back in the car, Ronald noticed he had a text message from Asia. "Hey, Ronald! Don't worry about stopping by my house on the way home. Chloe and I are heading to your house for dinner tonight. Joy just called and invited me over."

Ronald smiled and turned to Tyler and said, "Your aunt is coming over for dinner tonight. I don't know what it is, but sounds like she and your mother are up to something."

"Yes, but I like when Aunt Asia comes over, so I'm sure it will be fun. Also, I'll be able to tell her about my day on the golf course." Tyler said.

"Yes, you're right. I enjoy having Asia around too. When the two of them put their heads together, they typically come up with something good."

When they pulled up to the house, they saw Asia's silver car in the driveway. Ronald said to Tyler, "Well, your aunt beat us home. And her car is pretty dirty. Maybe we'll have some time before she leaves to wash it for her. You think she will appreciate that?"

"Yes, her car is dirty for sure, but so is your truck. I think we need to wash them both."

"Good point, Son. We don't want to drive to church in a dirty truck tomorrow. But you didn't have to call me out like that," Ronald smiled and said.

Ronald parked his dirty truck in the driveway next to Asia's equally dirty car. Once parked, Tyler hopped out of the truck, and put his golf clubs and shoes away in the garage. They both then walked in the house where they were warmly greeted by Chloe, who was happy to see her daddy and brother back home.

"Hi, Chloe, did you miss us?" They both said, as they each gave her a hug and a kiss.

Ronald then walked into the kitchen where he saw Asia and Joy unpacking groceries.

Ronald said, "Hello, we're home…. Oh boy, what's going on in here? Crab leg clusters, lobster tails, shrimp, sausage links, yellow corn, red potatoes, sticks of butter, Old Bay, and the large pots on the stove?"

Joy just looked up and smiled.

Hearing his dad name the items he saw in the kitchen, Tyler yelled out from the next room.

"Crab boil!"

This was another one of Tyler's favorite dishes. He had tasted a low country boil for the first time last summer while visiting an uncle in South Carolina. He'd instantly fallen in love with the dish. In addition to being delicious, it also lent itself to great family gatherings and conversations while everyone collectively cracked and sucked crab shells, bit into juicy sweet yellow corn, and filled up on sausage and potatoes.

Joy responded to Tyler saying, "Yes, we're making a low country crab boil. Asia and I were anxious to hear about your time on the golf course, and she saw an ad that the store was having a sale on seafood. We thought since it's a nice evening, we could make a crab boil. I have a few large pans, so I figured we could put everything in them and spread it out on the table on the back deck. How does that sound to you, Tyler?"

"Oh, that sounds like good eating. I can't wait!"

"I thought you might like that idea. Well, we're just getting started so you have time to shower and relax for a while. I'll need you and your dad to clean off the table on the back deck for us though."

Loving a good crab boil, Ronald then said, "I think that's a great idea too. Tyler and I were going to wash the truck and Asia's car. So, Son, go ahead and change clothes and we'll quickly wash them, then clean off the deck. By the time we do that, the food will be ready.

"Oh wow, you two are going to wash my car? It really needs it. Thank you Brother and thank you Nephew."

Tyler said, "Yes, Aunt Asia. Sure, Dad, that sounds like a plan."

Joy told them, "Well you guys hurry up if you're going to do all of that, no one likes cold seafood."

Tyler ran to his room to get changed, and shortly after, he and his dad headed out to wash the vehicles and clean off the deck. Just as the two finished cleaning off the deck, and putting out the plates and drinks, Joy and Asia were ready to bring the food out.

"Wow!! Everything looks so good. I'm ready to dig in," said Tyler.

"Well thank you, Son. How about you say grace so we can eat while it's still hot," Joy said.

Without missing a beat, Tyler said grace, and the family all dug into the pans of food. Tyler went for the crab legs first, while Chloe took a big bite out of the red potato that was placed in front of her.

"So, Nephew, let's hear it, how did your day on the golf course go?" Asia asked.

"It was awesome. The golf course was beautiful; the grass, the scenery, even the weather was perfect. I think I played well for my first time out. I mean I still have a lot of work to do to improve my putting and consistency, but Coach Jackson said that will come with time and practice."

"So, are you satisfied with how you played? Did you enjoy the time out there?"

"I did enjoy being out there. Like I said, it was beautiful, and it was good to see the difference between hitting balls at the range versus on the golf course. But, I wasn't satisfied. I have more work to do. It was good for my first time, but not good enough to win. I want to be the best."

"It was your first time out. Do you think you're being too hard on yourself?

"No, I'm not. It felt good to play on the course. I just know where I want to go, and I am willing to put in the work."

"Okay. What do you think you're going to need to do to get where you want to be?"

"Well, I am definitely going to continue my morning practicing. I think that has been helpful. Also, when possible, after I am done with my homework I'm going to get in a few more swings. If we can, I want to start getting to the range a little early to work on my putting. I'm also going to check out a few of the golf videos on YouTube that Coach Jackson told us about."

"Well, it sounds like you have a real plan. My nephew is a golfer." Asia said excitedly, with a big smile.

Ronald then spoke up and said, "Well, I'll say this first, ladies this crab boil is slamming! It's a party in my mouth. Tyler is being hard on himself because he has goals, which I understand, and respect. However, I have to say it was something special for me to get to be there and watch him play. Let me tell you, the first ball I watched him hit, oh boy! Tyler stepped up to the ball, his swing was smooth, and that ball took flight like it had wings. It soared up above the trees as if to survey the course from a bird's eye view. Then it picked a perfect spot on the green to come in for a soft landing just a few feet from the hole. Let me tell you it was great, like a work of art! I was some kind of proud of my son."

"Oh, Tyler, that sounds amazing. I look forward to seeing you play soon. That's my boy!" Joy said.

"Thank you, Mom and Dad. Mom, it will be nice having you and Aunt Asia there soon," Tyler said.

Asia told Tyler, "Well I look forward to getting to watch you in person soon, too. I love that you have a plan that you're already executing, and I know you'll continue. As for today, thank you both for washing my car, and I'm happy you're enjoying the boil. Eat up, there's plenty left."

The family continued enjoying their delicious meal, and good family conversation. As it started to get late and the cleanup was done, Asia said, "Well family, it's getting late. Joy, thank you for the invitation, this was a great idea and an even better meal. If I'm going to make it to church tomorrow, I have to head home and get some sleep."

"Asia, thank you for coming over and helping me cook. I'll give you a call during the week."

Sunday Church Service

The next morning before church, Tyler was up an hour early again and in the back yard taking practice swings. At breakfast that morning, Joy said to Tyler, "I didn't know you were going to practice this morning too. You weren't tired or sore from practice and playing yesterday?"

"I was a little tired, and I could feel a little tightness from yesterday, but taking a few swings this morning helped me to loosen up. I feel good now. I can't wait to see Deacon Chapman today and tell him about my time on the golf course."

"Okay, well don't overdo it with the practices. You have to take care of your body. I'm sure that Deacon Chapman will love hearing about your golfing experience."

When the family arrived at church, they were a little early, so Tyler was able to see and speak to Deacon Chapman before the service.

"Good morning, Deacon Chapman."

"Good morning, Tyler! How are you this morning?"

"I'm doing well. I told you that I have been taking golf lessons, well yesterday I got to play on an actual golf course."

"Oh, that sound great, Tyler. How did it go? How did you play?"

"I did okay for my first time. It's certainly different than hitting balls at the driving range. The fairway is a lot more narrow than the driving range, and on the course, every swing counts."

"Haha. Tyler you're correct, on the course is very different than at the driving range. How did your experience on the golf course make you feel about the game? Do you think it's something you will want to continue with?"

"I felt good about it. I have a lot of work to do because I want to be great, but I did enjoy my experience. It was also good to have my dad there with me."

"Well, that is great to hear, Tyler. Remember golf is a game with a lot to master. It's more than just which club to use and when. You have to know how to use that club in different situations, how different weather conditions will affect your ball, and how just the slightest inconsistency in your swing or how you hold the club, can impact the ball. My point is, if you want to be great at this, as you've already said, you'll certainly have to work hard at it over a decent period of time. Even then you'll still have parts of your game that you will need to improve on. Just give yourself some grace as you work to get there. What I mean is, push yourself hard, but forgive yourself when you don't master it immediately.

"Thank you, Deacon Chapman, that means a lot and I needed to hear that."

At that time, the music started to play, indicating that the service was about to begin. Once again, the sermon was powerful and seemed to resonate directly with Tyler and his new experiences. By the end of the service, it was clear that Ronald was proud of his son, and had been making his rounds to tell several members. Shortly after the benediction, Deacon Jones, Deacon Smith, Mother Kenny, and the music director, all came up to Tyler to say, "Congratulations on your golf game. Your dad said you looked really good out there. Keep it up." Tyler was appreciative of the encouragement, but like always, was puzzled at how his dad was able to speak to so many people, so quickly.

In addition to the other members that Ronald got to speak to, Deacon Chapman made it a point to speak with Ronald as well.

"Ronnie, how are you this morning?"

"Hello, Deacon Chapman. I am blessed. How are you today?"

"I'm doing well, thank you. I got to speak with Tyler this morning. Sounds like things are progressing with his golf game. He told me about getting to experience the golf course yesterday. He seems really excited to be playing and improving, but I know you already know that. What I wanted to make sure you knew, is that he really enjoys you being there. That's important to him. He didn't directly say it, but he said enough! I know how much you were there with him and encouraging him with basketball, you have to make sure you're also there for him with golf. This is important to him, and he has to know it's as important to you as well."

"Deacon Chapman, you are correct. I have noticed that, and he's shared that he enjoys having me there. I want to thank you for our previous conversation. That combined with some research Tyler did on the game, has me feeling a lot better about him playing and being prepared for any challenges he may face. I'm proud of him and grateful for you and our conversations."

"Ronnie, that makes me happy to hear. I'm proud of you. Hey, speaking of our last conversation, here is the contact information for Gill. Gill is the person my old investment guy, Nate, referred to me, for you. Nate told me he worked in the same office with Gill before retiring and handed over many of his clients to him. Give him a call."

"Thank you, Deacon Chapman. I'll give him a call this week to set up an appointment."

A Team Of Our Own

At lunch the next day, Tyler and Ryan sat together as they did most days, and today the conversation was all about golf.

"Tyler, you're really getting much better with your golf game. It took much longer for Coach Jackson to take me out on the golf course with him, and my first time wasn't as good as yours."

"Thanks, Ryan. I'm really enjoying the game. It's certainly a big difference hitting balls on the range versus hitting them on the golf course. With all the trees, water, bunkers, doglegs, and high grass, it was really different."

"Yeah, but you adjusted well. That's what I struggled with too, even this past Saturday. My hybrid is my go-to club when I'm in difficult spots, like high grass or around a lot of trees. You seem to be able to still use your irons well, in almost any situation."

"I need to get more comfortable with my hybrid. When I practice in the mornings, I spend most of my time with my irons and driver. I'll start working with my hybrid more."

"You're making me want to practice in the mornings. I just can't get up that early. How do you do it?"

"I don't know, I guess it's because I'm driven. I want to learn the game, and I want to be great at it. When

I did my research, and got to hear Coach Jackson's story, I just got really motivated. Knowing about some of the sacrifices people have made, and the challenges other golfers faced and overcame for me to have the opportunity to play; I have to make the most of it."

"Yeah, I get it. I just don't know if I can get up that early," Ryan laughed.

"Hi, Ryan and Tyler," said a voice from behind them. It caused both boys to briskly turn around to see who was calling their names.

"Lisa," exclaimed, Tyler and Ryan.

"Lisa, I didn't know you went to school here," said Tyler. Ryan added, "Neither did I."

"Yes, I'm a sophomore here."

"Really, a sophomore? That's wild, we've never met you before," Ryan said.

"Yes, well my family relocated here from out West for my dad's job at the beginning of the school year. I haven't met a lot of people yet, but when I saw the two of you on Saturday, I knew I'd seen you at school before. I just did not want to make an awkward situation because I knew we'd never spoken before.

"Oh, that's cool, you should have said something," Tyler said.

"No, I knew that I would see you today at lunch. This is my friend Suni, do you mind if we join you?"

"Sure, please do," Ryan responded.

"Hello, Ryan and Tyler right?" Suni asked.

"Yes, I'm Tyler and this is my friend, Ryan."

"Suni, Tyler is the guy I was telling you about. He's a beginner, but he's really good. Ryan is good too. They would be great for our team."

Ryan said, "Team? What kind of team?"

Suni responded, "I play in a co-ed golf league. We play a 6-week league on Saturday afternoons. There is a new season starting up, and the team I played on last year isn't coming back. Two of the kids moved away, and the other just said he wasn't playing any more. I told Lisa about it and she was interested, and told me about the two of you."

"A league? I'm not sure I'm ready for that. I'm still learning the game. Also, we take lessons on Saturdays," Tyler said.

Lisa told him, "Yes, it's on Saturdays after practice. So, for 6 weeks after practice, instead of playing the par 3 course with Coach Jackson and Coach Donna, we would play 9 holes on the big course on the other side of the range."

"Yes, and it doesn't matter that you're a beginner. In league play, you will have what's called a handicap. Your handicap is a way to balance the competition and keep the game competitive for everyone. Instead of you competing stroke for stroke against everyone, each player is given a handicap based on their skill level and average scores. As a beginner, you would have a higher handicap to start, which would adjust as you improve. In fact, continuing to improve your handicap may help the team more than hurt." Suni explained.

"I have heard of a handicap, but I didn't understand it or know what it was. I guess that makes sense. But, I don't know about a league. I'll need to speak to my parents and Coach Jackson about it. I want to continue to get better, and I'm sure competition will help. I just don't want to hold the team back by being the worst player, even with the handicap," Tyler said.

Ryan told Tyler, "I think playing in a league would be fun, especially with us having a handicap. It will even out the competition for everyone. Besides, you've been doing all of that practicing, and I've heard you say you want to be great. Here's your chance. Go Fore It!"

"Okay, I'll speak to Coach Jackson about it at practice to see what he thinks. Suni, how soon do you need to know my answer, and when will the league start?"

"The league will start in 2 weeks. I'll just need to know if we'll have a team by Wednesday of that week."

"Sounds good. I'll let you know before then."

Lisa said, "That will work. Well, I hope you decide to play. I think you're playing well for a new player, and it will be fun for us to all be on a team together."

"Yes, I think it will be fun too!" exclaimed Ryan.

"Well until then, you two should join us for lunch. Ryan and I meet here every day."

"I know, I have noticed you both here often," Lisa responded with a smile.

The four new friends continued to enjoy their lunch and get to know each other. Lisa shared some interesting stories about growing up out West, and Suni did the same about her experiences traveling to visit her grandparents in Beijing. The four enjoyed getting to know each other so much, they were almost late getting back to class for their next period. Before leaving, the foursome agreed to meet at lunch the next day to continue the conversations.

It was a slow day at the shop, so Ronald took the opportunity to come home a little early and was outside shooting basketball when Tyler came home from school. When Tyler got off the school bus and started walking up the street, he could hear the basketball bouncing. As he walked closer to the house, he noticed it was his father, home and in the driveway shooting baskets.

"Hey, Dad. What are you doing home so early?"

"Hey, Son. It was a slow day at the shop and the guys could handle it, so I decided to knock off a little early. I got here and just felt like shooting around. Come shoot a few with me."

"Okay, let me put my stuff down and I'll beat you at a quick game of horse."

"Haha-Haha, one thing is incorrect with that sentence. It will be quick, but you won't beat me. Don't forget I taught you everything you know, but you don't know everything I know."

With a smirk, Tyler said, "Very funny. But you did teach me that he who laughs last, laughs best. So don't laugh too early. Here, let me get in a few warm-up shots."

"I like the confidence, young man. Here you go, take the ball and get loosened up. How was school today?"

"School was pretty cool today. Do you remember that girl Lisa that we played golf with on Saturday?"

"Yes, I remember her. She was really good."

"Yes, her. She goes to my school. She and her friend Suni came and had lunch with Ryan and me today."

"Oh, I didn't know she went to your school. It didn't seem like you knew each other. Did you know she went there?"

"No, I did not. She came over to us today and introduced her friend. She said when she saw us, she knew we went to school together, but didn't want to make an awkward situation at golf."

"Awwww, so the young lady you and Ryan play golf with on Saturdays came and introduced herself, and her friend, to you and Ryan at lunch. Hum Uhmm," Ronald said, with an inquisitive smirk.

"Yes, but no Dad, it was not like that."

"Like what?"

"I know what you're thinking. They were telling us about a golf league that Suni plays in. Suni is Lisa's friend. She plays in this league on Saturday afternoons, but the team she played on last season has broken up."

"Humm, let me get this straight. Lisa and Suni invited you and Ryan to play in a league with them, and you're still learning the game, but they want you on their team anyway? But it's not 'like that', whatever that is? I hear you," Ronald replied, still with the same inquisitive smirk on his face. "Give me the ball, let's get this game started." Tyler gave him the ball and he took his first shot.

"I told them I was a beginner, and Lisa has seen me play. Suni explained the handicap system to me. It's how they adjust your scores to put everyone on an equal playing field, based on your average scores."

"Missed shot, that's H for you. The handicap, I understand that. A similar system is used for bowling leagues. Your grandfather and your great aunt both used to do a lot of bowling in leagues, so I understand that process. In fact, if you continue practicing and improving the way you are, you really could be a help to the team if you outpace your handicap average."

"Yes, that's what Suni said too. I know I'll continue to get better, because I am going to keep practicing. And Dad, that's H for you too."

"I can't believe I missed that shot! So, how will you play in the league on Saturdays, and still go to practice?"

"The league plays in the afternoons, so it's after practice. It's at the same time I would typically be on the course with Coach Jackson and Coach Donna. I want to ask Coach Jackson about it this week at practice. The league doesn't start for another 2 weeks, so I have time to get back in touch with them about if I'll play. Oh yeah, that is H.O., for you."

"Okay, I see you came to play today. That's a good idea to speak to Coach Jackson about it and see what he says. Oh man, I missed another one. You got lucky with that shot."

"Yup, my dad once told me, 'I would rather be lucky than good any day.' That is H.O.R., Dad."

"Touché. Well for what it's worth, I think you should play in the league. I believe competition brings out the best in athletes. It pushes you to dig deeper than you would ordinarily dig, you can learn from the other competitors, and it forces you learn how to focus singularly and block out distractions. All great traits that will serve you well throughout life's journey. That's H.O., for you, young man.

"Yeah, I like to compete. My only concern is if this is too early. I still have so much more to learn. I don't want to get overly frustrated seeing other kids perform better and do things I can't yet."

"That's my point, you'll learn from the other kids. How they approach certain holes, how they hit the ball to get out of different situations, or simply to set up the next shot. I imagine it's like basketball or football. Throughout the game you're running a series of plays to see how players respond, to set up the play you really want or need to run later. Or better yet, like chess, where you have to think a few moves ahead. In golf, you have to set up your second shot with a good tee shot. Unfortunately, I won't be able to show you how to do it, but you will be able to discuss it with Coaches Jackson and Donna, and I'm sure they'll get you right. Until then, that is H.O.R., young man. Don't call it a comeback, I've been here for years. Haha-Haha-Haha."

"Man, I can't believe I missed that shot. Yes, I get your point about competition. You know I hate to lose, so it will defiantly drive me to work at my craft."

"Yes, I know it will push you to work at your craft. Now, the ugly side of competition is that it can also bring out the worst in some people. Either because they don't know a better way to deal with losing, or because they don't feel you belong there in the first place. In healthy competition, it's where you experience some friendly trash talking like we're doing right now. You might experience some banter that's not very friendly, and in that type of competition, is where you may experience different forms of racism on full display. Speaking of competition, that's H.O.R.S., you're about to lose this little competitive game.

"I understand that. There was a lot of trash talking in our basketball games that the referee didn't hear. Guys like trying to get in your head. Uh-oh you left the door open with that missed shot. It is time for me to tie up this game of HORSE."

"Exactly, there's plenty of trash talking in basketball and it's all about getting in the other guy's head. If he's thinking about you, he's not thinking about what he's supposed to be doing, the play he's supposed to be running. As a result, he gives up a competitive advantage to the other person. While I didn't teach you to talk trash, you clearly picked it up along the way. However, what I did teach you was the importance of blocking it out, and letting your play do the talking. When you really start beating a trash talker, they often times will double down on the talk. At that time, one of two things will happen. One, the trash talking will get in your head and you lose focus, or two, the talking will have no effect on you, but will cause the opponent to lose focus on the game because they're focused on you. In which case, you win. BOOM! Just like I won this game H.O.R.S.E.! Hahaha! Good game Son, you did make it close there at the end."

"Man! I thought I was going to get you today. Thanks, Dad, that was fun."

"You came close, but you haven't mastered the bank shot like your old man. I told you, I taught you everything you know, but you don't know everything I know. On a serious note, do you get what I am saying about competition bringing out the ugly in some people? Especially in golf, you're very likely to hear or see some things that you know are just not right, and how you respond to it will be important. In some cases, no reaction is the best action. Let your play speak for you. You know the type of man you are and want to be. You don't have to prove your manhood every chance you get. Also, they'll be expecting you to overreact, so they can use it as justification for their point of view."

"I understand. Thanks for the game and the talk. I'm going to say yes to the league, I need to start my journey.

"I think that is a good decision. Still, talk to Coach Jackson about it to make sure we aren't overlooking anything. Now, let's head inside and get cleaned up. Your mother will be here with Chloe soon, and she's picking up dinner on the way home."

That week at his golf lesson, Tyler told Coach Jackson about the invitation he received to play on a league team.

"Tyler, that is a great idea. Personally, I think it's great to play with other kids to see where your skillset is compared to theirs and highlight areas for improvement for your own game. It's unusual for someone just starting to play the game to get invited to join a team. Typically, people look for players that are experienced, and already have their handicap. Do you know someone with a team?"

"Yes, Lisa, who played with us last week, actually goes to school with us. She and her friend, Suni came to talk to Ryan and me about it at lunch on Monday. Suni has played in the league before, but her team is not coming back. She is looking to start a new team with me, Ryan and Lisa."

"Okay, Tyler, Lisa is inviting you and Ryan to play on a team with her and a friend? Nice! Lisa has been playing really well over the last few months. I think it will be great for all of you to experience the larger course, and see a little competition. I just want you to make sure you keep it in perspective that you're still a beginner. There will be times that you'll hit a few bad balls in a row. You'll have to be careful not to start overthinking every swing. You will need to have what I call a short memory in between shots. Meaning, no matter how good or bad the previous shot was, focus on the swing you're about to make, the shot you're about to take.

"Yes, that's my one big concern, not playing well and hurting the team. Lisa's friend, Suni, did explain to me how the handicaps work, so that made me feel a little better. I'm going to continue to practice every day, so I know I'll keep getting better."

"I know you will. What I didn't know was that we were making a love connection on the golf course last week. I'll have to tell Coach Donna that her student might have made a connection."

Blushing, Tyler said, "No, Coach Jackson, it is not like that. It's about golf."

"Okay. Golf."

The Good, The Greats and The Ugly

With the positive feedback from his dad and
Coach Jackson, Tyler did decide to join the team and play
in the league. Over the 6-week league season, all four
players on this newly formed team played well and
improved each week, but none more than Tyler. His
continued commitment to his morning and evening
practices, watching videos Coach Jackson suggested for
him, and the additional work he did practicing his putting
and getting out of bunkers at the range, had been paying
off greatly. That work, coupled with his high handicap at
the beginning of the season, proved to be the team's
secret weapon and advantage. So much so, that they got
to play a 7th week to break a tie between them and two
other teams for the league championship.

For this championship match, Tyler, Ryan, Lisa,
and Suni all came into the weekend playing some of their
best golf of the season. They were feeling good, and were
confident they would be competitive in their pursuit of a
championship. For this match, each player had their
parents there to support the team, including both Coach
Jackson and Coach Donna. Also in attendance were Aunt
Asia, Deacon Chapman, a few members from the church,
and Carrie from the Café. Ronald, as always, has been
extremely proud of his son's progress and success, and
has shared it often, including inviting the church to come
support the team. While this was simply a league
championship with no national ranking, no cash prize,
and not even a trophy, it was a defining moment for this
newly formed team and in Tyler's personal growth and
golf journey. For Deacon Chapman, it was meaningful

for another reason. It was the realization of generational progress that had made it possible for a team consisting of 2 Black boys, a bi-racial girl, and an Asian girl, to step on a golf course and compete against 2 other teams of White boys and girls for a league championship. No matter who won, it was a proud day for them all.

Before the match, the 12 players got a chance to interact, some meeting for the first time, while others picked up from previous interactions. In the group setting, everyone was cordial and wished each other good luck. However, as the teams began to separate and head towards their carts, one player was heard saying, "No way we are losing to team United Nations over there." As that player's teammates laughed, another said "You mean team Tiger Woo?" That comment was followed by more laughter. "Yeah, not sure how they got here, but we'll show them where they belong." Ryan, having heard enough, turned towards the direction of the comments and said, "Excuse me!"

Tyler quickly reached with his left hand to grab Ryan's arm and continued walking in the direction of their cart, at the same time saying, "Ryan, no! We'll let our game speak for us. Stay focused."

Tyler then turned his head over his left shoulder in the direction of the comments, waved his right hand over his head and said, "Thank you, good luck to your team as well."

The other team continued to laugh and waved back as they walked towards their cart.

Ryan, frustrated with not getting to address the racist comments clearly hurled their way, looked at Tyler and said, "Why did you do that? Why did you let them get away with that? You heard what they said. We can't just let them get away with that. We should have done something."

"Ryan, I get it, but we were the only people that heard it. It would have been our word against theirs. We potentially wouldn't have gotten to play this match. They did that to get a reaction out of us. They want us thinking about them and what they said, and not our game. To be honest, that tells us they're afraid they might not be able to beat us. What we can't do is fall into their trap. We can't lose focus and start thinking about them more than the championship. That's what they want and I have no plans of giving them anything that they want. I plan to just beat them and win the championship. I'll tell you something, when I'm faced with people trying to get me off my game, I sing this song in my head:

No weapon formed against me shall prosper,
it won't work.
God will do what He said He will do.
He will stand by His word,
He will come through.

No weapon formed against me shall prosper,
it won't work.
God will do what He said he will do.
He will stand by His word,
He will come through.

Singing that gets me refocused and prepared. Ryan, are you good?!"

"I get it Tyler, you're right. I'm good. Let's go get this 'ship!'"

"That's what I am talking about! Lisa, Suni, are you okay?"

"Yes," said Suni.

"Yes, I am fine. Thank you for the pep talk and for keeping us focused. I came today to win, but now I really want to beat that team!" Lisa said.

Tyler responded, "Yes that's the spirit! But, I do have one question... what should our team name be? We were just Team 6 throughout league play. When we win this championship, I want them to call us something better than Team 6."

"When the time comes, we trust you'll know what to say," said Lisa, to which everyone agreed.

The teams headed off to their respective starting holes for the shotgun start; that meant each team started at the same time, at a different hole on the course. For Team 6, they started at the second hole, which was a par 3.

"Here we are! Lisa, you're up first. Start us off right." Tyler said, as he stepped out of the cart and began putting on his glove and grabbing his 7 iron.

Lisa stepped out of her cart, adjusted her visor and slid her glove on her left hand. She looked at the marker to take note of the distance to the hole and made sure she'd grabbed the right club. She then reached into her bag to get a ball and a tee. She walked up to the tee box, put her tee in the ground and placed the ball on top. She took a few steps back to stretch. She looked at the flag to take note of the direction of the wind, and once more adjusted her visor. Stepping up to the ball, she said, "Here we go." She addressed the ball with her club, took one last peek at the flag, then her eyes were back on the ball. She began her back swing, then forward, and Ping! The ball took flight.

It was a beautiful first shot from the tee. It was straight as an arrow as it soared across the sky like it had no plans of ever coming back down to earth. After what felt like a few minutes of flight, the ball finally began its descent like it had a radar locked in on the base of the flag and the middle of the hole. As if Lisa controlled the ball with a remote, it came in for a landing 3 feet away from the hole, rolled backward towards it, and came to rest just 6 inches away. It was the most beautiful shot she had ever hit. The entire team congratulated her on an extraordinary start to the championship match. It was just the first of several beautiful shots hit by the entire team. Suni, Tyler, and Ryan all had an extraordinary day on the course. Every shot was where it needed to be, and for the ones that were a miss, a great recovery shot was made. Team 6 owned the day.

When the three teams finished their round, the only question was which team finished second and third, because Team 6 was the clear championship winner. They'd beat the second-place team by 7 strokes. The PA announcer walked over to Tyler, Ryan, Lisa, and Suni to ask, "I'm about to announce the winner, do you have a team name other than Team 6?" Everyone looked at Tyler, and Tyler at each of them.

"You really want me to name the team," he asked?"

They all answered, "Yes."

"We are Team Peerless!"

The announcer confirmed, "Peerless, are you sure? What does that mean."

Tyler responded, "Well, look around. There is no other team out here that looks like us. There is no other team that has improved above our handicaps as much as we have. And there's no one that can tell our story like we can. We are without peers. Peerless!"

"Okay, I get it." The announcer took the mic, thanked everyone for coming out, and thanked the players for their participation in the league. Then he said, "Today we would like to recognize Team 9 as our third-place team. We have Team 12 as our runner up. And a big congratulations to our league champions, "Peerless," formally known as Team 6."

The parents and spectators there to support Team 6 all stood, cheered, and applauded the team's success. The 4 players exchanged high fives and hugs. It was a special moment for them all. Lastly, the time had come to shake hands with the other competitors. When approaching the team that had shouted the pre-match comments, Tyler took the lead, saying, "My name is Tyler. This is Suni, Lisa, and Ryan. Together, we are "Peerless," formally known as Team 6. Not the United Nations, but we are better together. Thank you for the match and the motivation in the beginning. Have a great evening."

With that, "Peerless" gave no more energy or thought to that team. They walked over to their family and loved ones to continue their celebration.

Aunt Asia was the first person to greet Tyler to give him a big hug and to let him know how proud of him she was. She was followed closely by Joy, Ronald, Carrie, Deacon Chapman, and the church members. Afterward, Coach Jackson and Coach Donna came over to congratulate the team as well. Coach Jackson told Tyler, "You have been holding back on me at the range. You hit some of the best balls I have ever seen you hit out there today. Keep up your practices and learning the game, you're well on your way to being the great player you want to be. Really nice stuff out there. But, now that I know you have it in you, I'm going to push you even harder to get your best to consistently come out. I'm proud of you!"

"Thank you, Coach Jackson. I look forward to you continuing to push me."

Just then, Lisa's dad headed toward Tyler and started trying to gather up the team. Once everyone was gathered around, Lisa's dad said, "Hello team Peerless. It is Peerless right? I like that name. My name is Rick, I am Lisa's dad. I want to say congratulations on a great season, and your big win today. You each played extremely well. I also want to thank you for befriending my little Lisa. I know moving here from out West wasn't easy for her. It's not what any teenager would want to do. However, your friendship has certainly made the transition much easier for her, and for us as a family. For that, I am extremely grateful. As a small thank you, and since you all are golfers now, I've got tickets for the PGA championship in Kiawah Island next month, from the 17th to the 23rd. My job is one of the sponsors. I would like to offer you and your parents tickets for whichever day you would like to attend. It would be a great experience for you. You would be able to see the greats do their thing live in person. If you're not able to answer me right now, you can just let Lisa know at school, what day and how many tickets you need. Once again, congratulations on today, and a big thank you for your friendship."

Everyone smiled and cheered as they thanked Rick for his generous offer. Tyler said, "Mr. Rick we're glad you and your family moved here and we got to meet Lisa. She is a great person and teammate. Without her, we wouldn't have this team." Team Peerless all came in for a big group hug.

Tyler then turned to his parents and aunt and said, "I want to go to the championship. Can we go?"

"Tyler, that's during your exam week. I believe you have tests that Wednesday and Thursday. Also, I am working that weekend and the beginning of that week," Joy said.

Asia responded "…Well, I'm still working from home, and could use a change of scenery. If you and Ronald are fine with it, I could take him down there for the weekend and that Monday's event. I can have him study for his tests some over the weekend, attend the tournament on Monday, and we can come home on Monday night or Tuesday morning. I mean "YOLOSWN?"

"How about that, Mom? What Aunt Asia said, she can take me? I will still be sure to get my studying in, and I will get this great experience of attending the championship. My experience at the tournament can be my first essay of the summer. How about it? Can I go?"

Joy looked at Asia with a certain, "This is against my better judgment," smirk, then looked at Tyler and said, "I'll let you go, but you and your aunt have to make time for you to study. You've had a great school year and I want to see you do well on your exams."

"That is awesome! Thanks, Mom!"

"Wait, I'm also going to take you up on your offer to write an essay about it as well. You need a few summer assignments, and I am looking forward to hearing about the tournament. I've never been to a PGA event, and I don't know anyone who has. I'm interested in experiencing it through you."

"You bet, I'll write the essay as soon as I get back and finish my exams."

Tyler walked over to Rick and Lisa, who had begun to walk away, and said, "Mr. Rick, I just worked it out with my parents, and I will be able to attend the event on Monday the 17th with my aunt. I would need 2 tickets. Is that still okay?"

"Of course, it's okay! I'll have Lisa email you the tickets. She'll be attending that Monday as well, and since I'll be working the event, maybe the three of you can connect and explore the course together," Rick replied.

"That will be perfect! I'm really looking forward to this experience."

The Church Family

For Tyler, Sunday at church was very reminiscent of going to school the day after hitting the game winning shots in the rivalry basketball game against the Cougars. When Ronald parked the car and everyone got out, one church member walking by said, "Tyler, I heard you're a wiz with a golf club. Keep it up, God bless."

"Thank you", Tyler replied.

Another said, "Hey Tyler, I was at the Café this morning for breakfast and Carrie was telling me about your golf game. That is very good, keep at it."

"Thank you, I will definitely keep at it."

The usher working the front door said, "Tyler, you did your thing on that golf course, you're a natural. God is blessing you."

"Thank you. Yes, He is."

Another member walking by simply said, "Hey there, Tyler, won't He do it."

"Yes, he will."

Lastly, Deacon Dawkins walked up to Tyler and said, "Watch out there now. Tyler, I heard you did your thing with that golf club. You whipped them. Keep it going. God is good."

"All the time."

"And all the time."

"God is good."

"Amen young fella! Be blessed!"

As the family took their seats and the service began, members continued to try to make eye contact with Tyler, to give him smiles, waves, nods, thumbs up, anything to acknowledge what he had done, and to encourage him to continue.

Unlike the attention he received when he hit the game winning shots in the basketball game, this time, Tyler embraced the experience. He knew how hard he had worked to excel at this sport. He understood the history of the game and the barriers that had to be broken to allow him the opportunity to compete. Prayerfully, he would compete at a high level one day. However, he wasn't prepared for what Reverend Brown did at the end of the service.

"Tyler, please come up to the front of the church, here at the altar," Reverend Brown said.

Tyler was completely caught off guard and was curious as to why he was being called to the front of the church, but of course, he got up and did as he was asked.

"You all know Tyler. He has grown up here in the church, right before our very eyes. Tyler is a good student, a Wilderness Scout, an athlete, and an all-around good kid. Tyler, I understand you have taken up the game of golf, and from what I hear, you're playing very well. Your team won a league championship yesterday, and you were a major contributor to the win. I am as happy as can be to hear about your success, and what God is doing in your life. I look forward to seeing you play in person real soon. Deacon Chapman, please come up to the front.

Tyler, I know you know Deacon Chapman, but you probably do not know that he was a great golfer in the United Golf Association, the UGA. Deacon Chapman enjoys giving encouraging words and sharing his wisdom, but he doesn't like to talk about himself and his accomplishments. However, I want you to know the resources and support you have right here. Ronald and Joy, come on up and bring Chloe with you. Now as they come up, I want everyone else to come up to the altar and surround Tyler and his family and join hands.

Tyler, I want you to know that God will not bring you to something that He will not bring you through. You have this entire church family and community in your corner. You have the opportunity to do something special. You have all of us pulling and praying for you. I also want you to know that some people will come at you. They will try to knock you off of your game. They will not want to see you succeed. They will try to make you feel you are not good enough. That you are less than or that you simply do not belong. That is why you must put on the full armor of God, so that when the day of evil comes, you may be able to stand your ground. Ephesians 6. You cannot allow the words of others to shake your foundation. What God has for you, it is for you. Amen. Please remain standing for the benediction."

Tyler was filled with emotion from the experience. He had seen the church gather to pray for members that were ill, or going off to war, or had been going through a really tough time. But never for him, not for a sport.

As everyone began to clear out at the conclusion of church, Deacon Chapman stayed so he could walk and talk with Tyler.

"Hey, Tyler, how are you feeling?"

"Deacon Chapman, I'm a little overwhelmed, but I feel good. You never told me that you played golf. Not only played, but that you played in the UGA. I learned about that league when I was researching golf. I think it is still active today isn't it? You had to be really good. You'll have to teach me a few things.

"Yes, the UGA is still active today as a nonprofit organization, and helping a lot of kids. I'll help you where I can, but you're already doing pretty well on your own. Especially where it counts, which is in your head."

"In my head? What do you mean?"

"Well, you didn't notice me walking by, but I heard what those other kids said to you all before the match. When I was walking back to the grandstands, I heard what they were yelling and saying to you and your teammates. I saw how you took your teammate and didn't allow him to respond. I understand the urge to respond, I was the same way. I was not going to take any junk from anyone, no cheating, and especially no racist comments or acts. But, I wish I'd had a friend like you to help me keep my temper in check, or that I could have been as strong mentally as you, to be able to walk away and let my game do the talking for me. I could play extremely well, but I didn't control my emotions as well.

Too often, I felt the need to respond to each slight, to prove my manhood to each person that challenged it. As a result, I was labeled as aggressive and not gentleman enough for the privilege of playing the game of golf at a competitive level. Now, I can only imagine what you said to them after the match. Whatever it was, they needed to hear it. I just want you to know I am proud of you. We are all proud of you. You have the opportunity to stand on the shoulders of those that came before you and blaze a trail for others to follow. Who knows, you may be blazing a path for Chloe right now."

"You're right. I didn't notice you there, or that you heard that. Those kids were just evil. Ryan was pretty hot, and I could tell Suni was uncomfortable too. I'm used to trash talking, and people wanting to get in your head from basketball, and my dad taught me how to handle that. The racial comments hit a little differently than simple trash talking. I thought about those comments the entire match, but I was determined not to let them win. I'm happy I had that experience then. Now I know that I can handle the situation, and still play my game. And win!

"Yes, you do. You certainly do know how to handle yourself."

What An Experience

It was the 17th of May and the day that Tyler was attending the tournament. After praying God's blessing on the food they were about to receive, and for traveling mercies over Tyler and Asia, Ronald looked up at Joy and said, "How do you think their day at the tournament went?

"I hope it went well. I spoke to Tyler yesterday to make sure he remembered to study. He and Asia both said that he had done a good amount of studying and was doing some reading then. He could not stop talking about his excitement for today though. Apparently, they went to a golf course Saturday morning, and out for dinner on Saturday night, and at both places, they met someone that was going to the tournament, had been to one before, or was a fan of golf, and wished they were attending. I could tell he was smiling from ear to ear."

"Yes, I spoke to him on Saturday and he was telling me about the person he met at the golf course. He was definitely excited. I'm happy and excited for him too. I was very skeptical about this whole golf thing. I couldn't understand it, and I didn't understand why he was so into it. I didn't want him to get let down, or hurt physically or emotionally. But I've learned a lot through this experience. I don't have to understand why he likes it so much, just understand that he likes it."

"Correction, he loves it."

"Correct, he loves it. It really isn't a bad sport. It looks like it can be fun, and looking at some of these golf courses, they're beautiful. You can't help but relax, enjoy the day and appreciate the beauty of God's work. You know, I've also learned a lot about our son. I thought sports just weren't his passion. It turns out, my beloved basketball just wasn't his passion. I also learned that he's mentally stronger and wiser than I realized. Part of my concern with golf was the history and the mistreatment I thought he might face. I was concerned how he would respond to it if it happened, and if his response would create more issues for him.

However, him doing that research, learning about the game the way he did, and asking the questions he asked, helped to prepare him. It also allowed us to help him fill in the gaps and support him through his journey. When Deacon Chapman told me about what happened at their league championship match, I was upset and wanted to address it with the league. But, listening to him explain how Tyler handled himself and supported his teammate really made me proud. While I wish those types of interactions never happened, I'm glad that when one did, Tyler was able to handle it. I know that our son will be able to handle whatever comes his way, wherever his journey takes him."

"I agree, and I am happy to hear you say that and feel that way. This has been a journey for you too. I know how your experiences have shaped your perception, and like anyone, your perceptions are your reality. However, times are changing. While not fast enough, or as genuine and authentic as they should be, they are changing. Today there's less in your face racism, and more microaggressions and systemic racism. Based on that interaction at his championship, we're supporting him and preparing him well for wherever his journey leads him."

"You're right, I agree with you wholeheartedly. I love you, Joy, and I love you too, Chloe, and I love you too, Son," Ronald said, as he blew each one a kiss, including a kiss in the direction of Tyler's empty chair.

"I love you too, Ronald," Joy said, as she blew him a kiss back. "I can't take it anymore; I'm calling Tyler and Asia. I have to know how today went."

Ronald laughed as Joy shoved her last piece of food in her mouth and reached for her phone to dial the number. "They will be back tomorrow."

"I know, but that's tomorrow, I want to know tonight."

After a few rings, Tyler answered the phone, "Hi Mom, the tournament was great!!!"

"That's why I'm calling. I want to hear all about it. I'm going to put the phone on speaker to let your dad can hear too, so don't leave out any details."

"Hi Dad! It was a long, exciting day. We're staying in the same hotel as Lisa and her dad, so we had breakfast with Lisa, since her dad had to be at the golf course early to help set up his work booth. We had to park in one of the big general parking lots because no one was allowed to park on the island at the event. They had these charter buses that took you from that parking lot onto the island and to the event. There must have been 80 or 100 buses. They were all over the place, making the 25-minute trips back and forth from the parking lot to the event. Once you got on the island, you saw big beautiful homes, perfectly manicured lawns, palm trees, and bodies of water with beware of alligator signs posted. I saw several holes of golf; I'm not sure if they were all the same course or different golf courses, but they were all perfectly manicured too.

Once we pulled up to the event, there was a big blue, orange and white sign that said, "Welcome to the PGA championship Kiawah Island Golf Resort Ocean course". It was official, we were at the tournament. Once we got inside, there were large booths set up. There was a credit card company, an investment company, a cell phone company and we saw Lisa's dad there with his company's booth. We took turns at the booth that was offering a free golf swing analysis, because why not learn from the professionals? Then we made our way over to the main concourse. This area was huge. There was a gigantic video screen that displayed the different players on the tour, different facts about the course, Q&As about past tournaments, and some videos. There was a big patio area that led up to the food bar. It was 9:00am and there were already a ton of people out there eating, talking, moving around and deciding what they would do next. There was also a model standing next to one of the luxury cars that a sponsor had out on display, and a bunch of trucks and trailers parked representing the different golf brands and sponsors. It was spectacular, you could feel the energy in the air.

Today through Wednesday are practice days for the golfers so there wasn't a schedule for who was playing when. You just had to walk around and see who you could see. So, we headed down to the first hole to see who was there. The first golfer we saw was hitting balls out of the sand. One after the other from the same spot, then from different spots, he was hitting ball after ball out of the sand. I was surprised to see just how much time a professional was spending hitting balls from one area. Then I noticed not only was he hitting the ball out of the sand, they were all landing within about a 5-foot circle of each other and only about 3-5 feet from the hole. In fact, a few times one ball would hit the other because they were all sitting so close to each other. Right then I understood, I was practicing the wrong way. When I practice getting out of the sand, my focus is to get out of the sand, just get it back on the grass. But, he was practicing to get the ball in the hole or as close to it as he could. I know I need to change my mindset, just getting out isn't good enough. I need to get the ball in the hole.

Then we walked up to the #1 tee box. We saw Ricky Fowler about to tee off. I was excited because I've seen him play on TV, and he's a good golfer. I got as close as I could in the crowd to watch him tee off. He took a few practice swings, then stepped up to the ball. As he did, the official raised the flag and the crowd got really quiet. He looked down at the ball, looked up at the fairway to visualize his shot, then looked back at the ball. With a powerful swing, pow, the ball was gone. The crowd cheered and oohed and 143wed at the flight path the ball took. Moments later, he, his caddie, and a guy I guess was his coach, all took off walking up the fairway to the ball to continue playing the hole. It was amazing to watch him tee off from so close. It was surprising for me to see just how close people are to the golfers while they played their round of golf. I would be nervous with so many people so closely watching me. I wondered how long it took him to get used to that feeling.

The way the course is set up, we couldn't walk up the fairway on that hole to keep watching him, so when the path was clear of golfers, we walked across the fairway on the 9th hole, to walk down to see others play on other holes. However, when the ropes were lifted and we were allowed to walk across, Lisa immediately noticed how perfect and soft the grass was that we were walking on. I did too, and I just thought… wow this is really soft grass. Lisa said, "I'm not sure this is just grass. It's so light and fluffy, I want to dive in and go for a swim." We both laughed and agreed, this was nothing like we'd ever walked on before.

We got to a spot where we were standing between the tee box for the 9th hole, and the pin, or the hole for the 8th. As we were standing there waiting for something to happen, it did. A ball just fell out of the sky onto the green of the 8th hole. We didn't see the golfer that hit the ball, but the shot was perfect. We started looking up the fairway on the 8th hole to find where the golfers were, and we spotted one about to take his shot. We watched as he seemed to effortlessly swung his club, and sent the ball sailing. We watched that ball travel through the air, and with the precision of a Triple Nickle Paratrooper, it landed on a spot even closer to the hole than the first ball. We were in awe. The skill you have to have to hit a ball that far, and that accurately is amazing.

Then we saw another golfer I recognized; it was Rory McIlroy. We couldn't get as close to him as we were to Ricky simply because of the hole he was teeing off on. But, he had a lot of people that were interested in seeing him take his shot. There was a buzz on that hole of the golf course, and in a few short moments, I understood why. When Rory hit the ball, he crushed it. I mean, it took off fast and flew high like it was piloted by the famed Tuskegee Airman. After hanging in the air for what seemed long enough for a cross-continental flight, the ball came down to a soft landing and slow roll to the middle of the fairway, ready for him to take his second shot. The crowd erupted with praise for the excellent shot, and ran to the area where the ball landed to see him take his next shot. Shortly after, he came walking down with a confident strut that only comes when you know you did your thing and did it well.

Next, was one of the highlights of the day for me. As we made our way to the 4th tee box, Ricky was just coming off of the 3rd hole. He and his group walked right past me, no more than 3 feet away. The way this tee box was set up, I was able to stand less than 10 feet away from him as he prepared and teed off on the 4th hole. That's something that would be completely nerve-racking for me, to have people that close to me as I take my shot. Just 10 feet away. But, I'm excited I got to be there, that I got to see it. I felt bad for the guy that shot after him. As he started his backstroke, someone's phone went off. The caddie seemed to have been mad and looked at the person with a death stare. It didn't seem to bother the golfer at all. He continued with his shot, which looked pretty good. I guess he was just in the zone.

After that, we had lunch and walked up the back nine holes. The highlight there was getting to see the 18th hole. It was special to see with the grandstands up, the sponsorship logos everywhere and the backdrop of the Atlantic Ocean. You definitely understand why the course is called the Ocean Course.

Of all the things that we saw and did today, the one thing I didn't see much of were people that looked like us. Outside of the 3 of us, we only saw eleven other Black people. We did not even get to see Harold Verner III, who is currently the only African American golfer in the tournament. Not getting to see, or maybe even meet Harold, was a little disappointing, but it gave me even more conviction in what I have to do."

"Really? What is that?" asked Joy.

"I have to take my focus and practice on my golf skills up another level, to put myself in position to be successful in this sport. Then, when I get on the tour, make sure I use my platform to introduce the game to more people from diverse backgrounds. And if I don't make it to the tour, because I know not everyone does, I have to be like Coach Jackson and introduce it to more kids. Golf should be for everybody, and I am going to Go Fore It!"

"Son, I'm happy to hear that this was an exciting experience for you, and I love hearing the conviction and passion in your voice. I know you are going to do great things and inspire a lot of people. You and your aunt enjoy the rest of your time there and have a safe trip home. I Love you!"

"I love you too, Mom. I love you too, Dad"

Ronald said, "I love you too, Son," and they hung up the phone.

Ronald and Joy looked at each other and said no words, they simply shared a smile. They knew their son was going to Go Fore It! in a big way!

The End

Discussion Exercises

- Tyler tried golf which was new to him, and at first he was not very good at it. Think about something you enjoy doing now, but were not good at it the first time you did it. What did you have to do to get better at it?

- Tyler discovered a passion for golf, and worked to get better at it. What is your passion? What are you currently doing, or what will you do, to bring it to life?

- In this story, Tyler has his parents, his aunt, Deacon Chapman, and a couple of good friends, Ryan, Lisa, and Suni as a part of his village. Who is in your village?

- There are a lot of great African Americans named in this book, how many did you know? Which ones are you going to look up and learn more about?

Essay Contest

In the story, Tyler had to complete an assignment, which was a 500 word essay. Complete Tyler's essay and submit it at www.goforeitusa.com to enter for a chance to win a prize. Submission and eligibility details are listed online. Go Fore It!

Golf Term Glossary

Birdie: Completing the hole in one less stroke than par.

Bogey: Completing the hole in one more stroke than par.

Bunker or Sand Trap: Sand filled pits along the fairway or near the green.

Dogleg: The bend to the right or left in the fairway.

Double Bogey: Completing the hole in two more strokes than par.

Eagle: Completing the hole in two fewer strokes than par.

Fairway: The stretch of short grass between the tee box and the green.

FORE: What golfers yell when they hit a bad shot, in the direction of other golfers. It alerts the other golfers of the potential danger.

Green: The area around the hole with finely cut grass.

Handicap: A number given to a golfer that represents their potential average score compared to par. This is designed to assist newcomers, and novice golfers.

Hazards: The trees, water, sand traps, and tall grass that create increased levels of difficulty to the hole.

Hole-in-one: Hitting the golf ball in the hole on your first stroke.

Hook: A golf shot that moves right to left for right-handed golfers, and the opposite for left-handed golfers.

Lie: The way the golf ball has come to rest after taking your shot. A good lie would be in the middle of the fairway. A bad lie would be in the long grass or on a hill.

Mulligan: An unofficial redo or second shot from the same spot.

Par: The number of strokes it should take for you to get the golf ball in the hole.

Pin or Flag: The marker used on the green to notify the golfer where the hole is.

Rough: Area of taller grass on either side of the fairway.

Slice: A golf shot that moves severely left to right for right-handed golfers, and the opposite way for left-handed golfers.

Stroke: The act of taking a swing with the golf club to hit the golf ball.

Tee Box: The designated area that marks the beginning of each hole.

Acknowledgements

I want to thank my village for investing in me over the years. Your support and positive reinforcement has meant the world to me. I have to specifically thank my Uncle Clarence "Dap Daddy" Robinson for giving me my first set of used golf clubs, and my friend Curtis Joe for suggesting we go to the driving range and use those golf clubs. Had it not been for the two of you, I may not have ever picked up this life-changing sport. Thank you to my sister and parents, for buying my first full set of golf clubs, which made me feel a little more comfortable going to the range, and start to consider going to a golf course. Thank you to JoAnne Venezia and Dale Korzec for inviting me to play and having the patience to teach me the game. You did not know this, but as I was learning golf, my father was battling cancer. The hours spent on the golf course with you were as much therapeutic, as they were recreational and relationship building.

Since learning the game of golf I have enjoyed several hours on some extremely beautiful courses, developed stronger relationships with friends and colleagues, and met some very interesting people. These are some of the amazing recreational, educational, networking, and career opportunities fostered through the game of golf. These are the experiences that I want to create awareness of with the Go Fore It! Brand. Visit www.goforeitusa.com to learn more.

Lastly, I have thanked my village already, but I have to thank you all specifically for this book. As I shared with each of you my purpose and vision for this book, and this brand, you were nothing but supportive. Even at times when I doubted myself or my progress, you encouraged me to keep pressing forward and to execute my plan. Had it not been for you, I am not sure this project would have ever been completed; certainly not on the timeline that I had set for it. To my Mother, Sister, Antwan, William, Kayla, Curtis, Freda, Karoline, and Jerome, thank you for the support, words of encouragement, being a resource, and positive energy! To my wife, Kimberly, a big thank you for all of the positive energy, encouraging words, redirecting my self-doubt, especially as the project came closer to completion, for creating quiet time and space for me to create, and for all of your artistic work on the book cover and website.

I am very appreciative of my village. I hope you, my readers, have a village just as supportive of you and your endeavors.

Go Fore It!
www.goforeitusa.com